Benjamin
Golden
Devilhorns

Benjamin Golden Devilhorns

Doug Shields

SALTIMBANQUE BOOKS

NEW YORK

Acknowledgements

Rebecca, if not you then none of this. Leah, you led me through a wormhole while Michelle reminded me to leave a trail of proper punctuation. And complete sentences. Eris, if you stop being weird, I'll murder you. Houston, you wizard. Islaya, you inspire me evil. Clayton, you proved that it's possible. Fury, just when I thought it couldn't be gotten, you got it. Dylan, Dylan, Dylan, the slow touch of human connection. Thank you. Mother, Dennis, Dad, Dianna: your sacrifices humble me.

Stories Inside

Benjamin
Golden
Devilhorns

Cocky Jockroach

Jay Gilbert Masterson, III owns more cockroaches than any other landlord in town. According to the health department, his cockroaches outnumber his human tenants by more than 11,000 to 1.

Jay once paid his illegitimate brother-in-law to fill the Ben Creek Apartments with a cloud of poison. The roaches stayed dead until a tenant's cloud of Cheetos evolved into a roach zombie virus. The undead roaches drug themselves from apartment to apartment, biting and reanimating their fallen comrades. The undead roaches could only be eliminated by decapitation or by direct contact with liquid roach killer. Jay now provides his tenants with aerosol cans and tells them to keep their walls wet with poison.

Masculinity is a point of pride for Jay. His gut hangs over his belt like no woman's belly ever could. His memory collects professional football statistics in the same way students on the Benjamin High School quiz bowl team collect *Star Trek* subplots. However, no matter how many times Jay coaches his Baby Boo Baseball team to victory, there is still a tiny part of his brain that is a Pussy.

The Pussy part of Jay's brain talks to him as he stands

outside a tenant's door in a brief moment of introspection after exchanging a can of aerosol bug killer for a rent check. The Pussy voice says, *Jay, aren't you asking your tenants to breathe poison—not just once, but every day, month after month? What if they get sick? There are children in this apartment. What if the children get cancer—or grow extra limbs? You'll feel bad then. And you'll get sued.*

Jay silently rebukes his Pussy voice: *The tenants don't have to spray if they don't want to. I'm not responsible for their choices. Besides, the human body is made of chemicals. I'm sure the body can find a use for—uh....* He pulls a spray can from the half-empty case, positions the can exactly eighteen inches from his farsighted face, looks at the active ingredients, and tries unsuccessfully to pronounce "imiprothrin". He then throws the can to the gravel and mumbles, "I hate cockroaches."

The only person in town who hates cockroaches more than Jay Gilbert Masterson, III is his son, Jay Gilbert Masterson, IV, known to everyone except his mother as Jock. His mother calls him Gilbert.

As a high school superstar, Jock Masterson's hate for cockroaches extends beyond the taxonomical class *insecta* to include most of his classmates. Just as he enjoys the art of dangling an insect over the mesmerizing flame of a stovetop until the heat forces him to let go, he also enjoys inflicting as much pain onto his peers as he thinks he can get away with.

For instance, Jay's second-favorite target is Floppy, a tenth-grader who should have begun shaving in eighth grade but didn't. Now his chin is overgrown with inch-long, very fine hairlets that flop when he talks. Jock likes to grab and twist Floppy's chin hair until Floppy screams "I'm an ever-flopping Gobflopper!" three times fast.

Unfortunately for Jock, Floppy is now on the football team. He plays third string wide receiver. The team only has two strings. Floppy is not allowed to play unless the team is at least forty points ahead, but he's still *on the team*. That means Jock can torture Floppy on the practice field or in the field house but never in the school proper. You can't tease a teammate in public. That's the rule.

So for in-school amusement Jock turns his attention to the pizza delivery boy named Dennis. Jock spends his creative thoughts devising new ways to make Dennis fall on his face. Walking every night with loads of imbalanced pizza boxes makes Dennis good at recovering from falls. Making Dennis fall is therefore a fun challenge for Jock.

At first Jock simply put his foot in Dennis's path, but that method quickly lost its entertainment value. One of Jock's newer methods is to shove or trip other people, sometimes two at the same time, and make them fall into Dennis.

Don't get the wrong idea. Jock isn't always mean to Dennis. In fact Jock is very friendly when Dennis delivers pizza to his house. Unlike the other pizza boys, whose pizzas are cooled to the point of solidification, Dennis always delivers his pizzas warm and stringy, no matter what. Jock enjoys Dennis's professionalism and basks in the otherworldly social experience when Dennis steps into his foyer. Last night Jock tipped 30%, a handshake, and a breathtaking smile.

Last night may have been pizza night, but this morning is a different day entirely. Today is restless in anticipation of the Homecoming game and dance. Tonight, Jock's own Benjamin High School, home of the Devilhorns, will play their blood enemy Garfield High School, home of the Holocaust. Today is the most pumped-up day on Jock's calendar. It is a day of celebration. A day to take Dennis's pain to a new level.

Dennis, for his part, only vaguely remembered that today is Homecoming when he arrived on campus. Now, as Dennis stands at the health room chalkboard drawing cartoons of dead politicians, Dennis doesn't form any thoughts of tonight's game, nor of Jock Masterson, who happens to be standing immediately to his right, grinning.

As Dennis's left hand draws Gerald Ford's forehead, Jock punches Dennis in the right arm.

Dennis stops drawing for a second. His weak Macho voice tells him, *Jock just hit you. That means you have to fight him. If he hits you then you have to fight. That's the rule,* to which his loud Pussy voice replies, *But look at his arms! He's muscular enough to throw power, slim enough to move quickly, and mean enough to—*

Jock punches Dennis's arm again.

Without thinking, Dennis returns the punch to Jock's arm. No damage.

A wide-eyed chorus of "Ooooooh" ascends from the seated students, who are now assured of a great show and an inside story to spread among the bleachers at tonight's game.

Jock snaps into a boxing stance. Facing him, Dennis stands stiffly with his feet together and his fists up. Jock throws a fist at Dennis's jaw. The fist connects.

Dennis's eyesight jolts. When his vision snaps back into focus, he finds himself on the floor. *I just got hit*, he thinks. *Hard enough to land on the floor. But, strangely, it doesn't hurt. Why doesn't it hurt?* Dennis gets back up.

The audience makes excited noises.

Jock resumes his stance, prancing from leg to leg, clearly having a good time. Dennis throws a fist at Jock's jaw. Jock dodges. Dennis throws another. Jock dodges again. Then Dennis rolls a solid volley, one empty punch after another. In all, Dennis attempts nine punches before Jock throws another fist into Dennis's face.

Again, Dennis finds himself on the ground. Again, no pain. *Why is there no pain?* Dennis gets to his feet.

The audience sounds like they're watching anal porn for the first time. A cacophony of "Oh my God," and "Dude, don't do it. Seriously!" and "That has got to be painful," spark the idea that maybe Dennis should change strategy.

When Dennis puts his fists up, Jock looks shocked. His eyes silently ask, *What—you want more? Seriously? Well, it's your face, not mine.* Jock resumes his stance and waits for Dennis to swing.

But Dennis doesn't swing. Instead, he points his shoulder toward Jock's stomach and lunges in a motion that one might use when tackling a lawn jockey. Dennis's arms wrap around Jock's waist as Dennis's momentum carries them both into a clutter of unoccupied desks. Jock's tailbone hits the ground.

Dennis is now hugging Jock. His neck is directly below Jock's armpit and his face is in a fortress of desk legs. If Jock had a knife he could bring the blade downward into Dennis's lower back but, being unarmed, Jock can only pound his fists onto Dennis's spine. Dennis finds that he prefers having his spine pounded to having his face pounded. He waits in this position for a teacher to arrive.

––––––––––––

Jock and Dennis are escorted to the chief authority's office. The chief authority determines that the school's no-tolerance fighting policy remains in effect no matter who threw the first punch. He therefore sentences each student to three days of suspension. He then calls the students' parents to give them the news.

Dennis's mother pleads for lenience on the grounds that her son had no choice but to defend himself. Jock's father pleads for lenience on the grounds that tonight's homecoming victory requires Jock's presence on the field. Woven in between Jay's words are two facts: 1) Jay charges the chief authority less than market value for his rental house, and 2) if the chief authority suspends Jock then Jay will whine about it at the next Kiwanis meeting.

The chief authority decides to show mercy to both parents by allowing Jock and Dennis to remain at school for the rest of today, and also to attend the Homecoming festivities tonight. Both students must then report to in-school suspension in the morning. Everybody happy? Dismissed.

––––––––––––

Dennis has never been particularly good at making friends.

But today, Homecoming Day, appears to be the beginning of a new social life. As soon as he leaves the chief authority's office, a queue of people approach him to offer solace and congratulations.

Floppy confesses his admiration to Dennis. "You did it!" he says. "You hit Jock Masterson. I've wanted to do that since fourth grade!"

A girl named Alison, whose black hair takes up more volume than her torso, introduces herself by kissing Dennis on the nose.

Even Jessica Lovelace, the shoo-in for tonight's Homecoming Queen, caresses Dennis's face with her baby-soft fingers, looks deep into the wells of his eyes and says, "Jock is such a prick."

All this before Dennis sees himself in a mirror.

When he finally makes it into the boys' room and stands in front of the glass, Dennis's reflection jolts him almost as much as the punches did. The blood from his nose is now caked onto his mouth and chin. His shirt is a star-chart of blood splotches.

The pain that previously stayed hidden now maps itself across his face. His nose and cheek feel like they are jabbing into his brain.

As Dennis surveys the damage, Jock Masterson walks into the bathroom. Dennis tightens. The two make eye contact with one another's reflections, each daring the other to look away. Time freezes.

Jock breaks the stare. He looks at the ceiling and makes his way into a stall.

Dennis blinks. *Wow,* he thinks. *Jock broke the stare. He can't hurt me anymore. Jock Masterson will never again treat me like a cockroach.*

Dennis returns to his bloody reflection. He looks into the eyes of an entirely new person.

Reading is Bad for You

It's the end of the story. You can't go on. Don't even try. I'm telling you, the next paragraph doesn't exist. Keep your eyes steady. If you look at the ellipse then you will go blind…

There. You're blind. What did I tell you? Ok, don't believe the writer. Just because fictionwriters can't keep real jobs doesn't make us ignorant. Think about the ignorance of writers next time you want to compliment your lover's outfit but you can't see it because you're blind. Or because you don't have a lover.

You don't have a lover because you read too much. Don't worry; you're not alone. Alison Graciously never had a lover, and she nearly went blind from reading. Her eyes waned slowly; she didn't notice her myopic vision until the doctor gave her magic lenses. Then she could see awhile. But soon her eyes grew tolerant of the lenses. Stronger prescriptions became less effective until Alison was in a constant state of lens tremors.

Alison's mother Grace begged her to quit reading. Find yourself a good husband, Grace pleaded, and then you can read all you want. But instead of dating, Alison spends her evenings with George Orwell, Anne Rice and *Star Trek: The Next Generation* authors. She intends to find herself a good husband but hopes that her husband will be made of words.

"Words don't pay the bills," Grace is fond of saying, although she doesn't believe it. Grace seeks opportunities to use words to get out of paying bills. Last November she bought a TV with her MasterCard and noticed that the cashier neither checked her ID nor made her sign the receipt, so Grace reported that her card had been stolen the previous day. She didn't have to pay. The practice is called *creative accounting*, Grace explained. Creative accounting is different than fictionwriting. Creative accounting is the poor man's way of getting back at the rich, while fictionwriting is the rich man's way of making the poor complacent, like TV only worse because reading makes you blind.

Ding Dong. Pizza boy at the door. His name is Dennis. Alison first met Dennis in Algebra II. Dennis likes to play with her hair. The first time he delivered pizza, Grace asked him if there were wedding bells in her daughter's future. Alison was so humiliated she locked herself in her room until she'd read the entire *Lord of the Rings* trilogy.

Dennis is the best pizza boy in town. His secret is the pile of small stones he keeps in the oven and places in the bottom of the pizza carrier before making his deliveries. His first attempt involved setting the pizza box directly onto the rocks. When he opened the carrier to take out the pizza, the box burst into flames. Dennis learned to place the pizza box on a rack in the carrier and let the rocks sit loosely underneath. His success is known countywide. Some clients refuse to order unless Dennis is delivering.

Dennis won't admit that he likes to read. He spends his lunch period on the basketball court trying to overcome his feet and limbs. Smooth, limber bodies guide the ball in and out of his reach. Dennis would rather be reading. His basketball buddies know it, Alison knows it—only Dennis remains in the closet.

Alison answers the door. She smiles and hands Dennis a crumpled ball of cash. Dennis gives her the change and a tattered paperback book. Startled, she holds the book to her face and studies the title, *2001: A Space Odyssey*. Wow! This book is on the upper half of her wish list. "What's this for?" she asks.

"Sorry I missed your birthday," he replies.

"My birthday's next month, goober."

"Oops." Dennis chuckles and blushes. With a sudden empathy, Alison reaches up and kisses him on the nose.

Spying from the kitchen, Grace lets slip a loud praise to Jesus.

Earl and the Gas-poop Sketty

Pickled bean sprouts are bad for digestion, at least according to Madeline McLeod, the whiskey grandmother who spreads her hands like a startled bat when pronouncing a diagnosis. "Gas!" she says. "Make you blow up like a wedding bird. You sleep on the couch."

Madeline's heart rattles when she watches *Judge Judy*, weekdays at four. Her eyes get narrow as she points at the screen. Skin dangles from her arm. She gives the television her highest commendation: "You tell 'em, lady!"

Earl McLeod stays in the garage during *Judge Judy*. His garage contains four lawn mowers, six sewing machines, a toaster, twenty-six shelves of tools, and a maze of free-standing cardboard. Last year Madeline wandered into the garage, got lost, and pressed her panic necklace. The ambulance reluctantly rescued her.

Judge Judy makes Earl nervous. Her squinty eyes and flying eyebrows smack Earl's soul. If Judge Judy and Madeline were drinking coffee together, Earl wouldn't stand a chance.

Earl has a daughter in Korea. She is old enough to be a

grandmother and Earl has never met her. When she was an infant her mother called Earl's house across the ocean. Madeline and the mother talked briefly. The phone slammed shut, leaving an after-ding that lasted for a full minute.

Madeline is usually unfocused. She starts to fry potatoes but gets lost cleaning the bathtub until the smoke alarm startles her back to reality. But when she watches *Judge Judy*, her mind focuses like a sniper hiding in the bushes for days or weeks, moving inches per day, eating bugs and inhaling the silence, waiting for a clear shot to fire an "Earl, did you stay up all night watching the TV again?" or an "Earl, you left the porch light on. I ain't made of electricity," or the big one, the bullet that has never been fired but still dreams of piercing Earl's skull: "Earl, you made a baby in Korea."

Five-thirty. Time to cook. Earl has made supper every Wednesday for the past decade as punishment for his affair with Ina Carol. Madeline gave no indication that she knew about Ina Carol until one Wednesday when Earl snuck into the house to use the toilet during *Judge Judy*. He emerged from the bathroom and saw a grapefruit hurling toward his head. "You poop!" His wife picked up another grapefruit. "I am a truth factory!" Earl slipped into the bathroom and, in a body-twist that left him sore for eleven weeks, crawled out the window.

Now Earl studies the pantry. He can fry better potatoes than Madeline but potatoes take too long. Spaghetti is quick and Earl would like to get rid of the jar labeled "meat sauce" that was canned in an unknown decade. So it's settled: spaghetti with meat sauce.

He steps into the kitchen. Madeline's voice: "Sushi called."

Earl freezes. He knows what she means, but he's obligated to ask.

Madeline replies, "Sushi. That oriental woman you gave birth to."

"Is that really her name?"

"Of course it is. I'm not the liar in this family." She picks up a grapefruit.

"Don't throw that grapefruit."

"You poop!"

"Don't throw that grapefruit." The last thing Earl sees is Judge Judy's eyebrows smacking the soul of a puffy freckled girl. Must be a marathon.

Earl wakes. His face is swollen and the window is dark. Madeline is holding a rosary over his face and chanting. She looks down.

"Earl!" Her eyes get teary. "My baby, I love my baby." She puts both hands on his cheeks and kisses his eyelid. "I'm sorry Earl, baby I did this to you."

Earl lifts his watch into view. Still Wednesday. Earl looks at the ceiling. Supper needs to be cooked. But the girl—"Madeline, did you get her number?"

"Yeah honey, I got it. Lemme go fetch it."

She ruffles into the kitchen, digs through the refrigerator, and wheezes. "Uh…" Her voice is shaky. "Oh…" The freezer door is open. Earl can hear the fan. "Earl, I think I lost it."

Earl sits up. Blood returns to his face. Pain.

Madeline from the kitchen: "I'm sorry, baby I did this to you."

Earl drags himself into the kitchen. Madeline hugs him. Earl softens and says, "It's okay, sweetheart. We'll find it."

Madeline wheezes and coughs her way into the living room.

Earl boils the spaghetti in silence. He mixes Madeline's serving with a heaping spoon of pickled bean sprouts. Madeline won't know the difference until she's blown up like a wedding bird. A vindictive smile makes its way across Earl's face.

———————

Midnight. The sheets smell like pickled bean gas. Earl leans his hand against Madeline's thigh. It vibrates. He slides his hand to her shoulder and kisses her scalp. "Madeline," he whispers. She mumbles part of a syllable. "Madeline, I'm sorry about…" He doesn't even know her name. "Sushi."

With her eyes still closed, Madeline lifts her head and touches her lips to his eyelid. The bed vibrates. Madeline whispers "you poop" and drifts back to the dreamworld.

When a Skull Cracks a Walking Stick

"Hey, Boom Back! Two more beers, *por favor*. Yeah, baby. Right here." Skizzy winks at the ink dragons seducing one another on the barkeep's neck.

"You might try paying your tab this time, Skizzy." Two full glasses hit the bar with a thud. Foam spills.

Skizzy returns his attention to Barley Hopps. "And then that evil woman, the Filch—" Skizzy chuckles at the cleverness of his insult—"the Filch kicked me out for no reason. No reason! Do you know why she kicked me out?"

Barley feels like he just woke up. He has heard this story from several people already. He looks into his beer and says, "She told me you were drunk and belligerent."

"Bull! I'd only had one beer." Skizzy rolls his eyes and takes a drink of his beer. "There was a homeless dude here at The Horndevil, and he had no place to go. It was cold, and he was in the bar looking for a place to stay—and I did what the Lord wanted me to do: I said *Hell yes I have a place to stay! Come sleep on my floor.* So he did. And in the morning I fixed him a nice breakfast—two eggs over easy and a piece of toast with mounds of butter. But when the Filch walked into my bedroom—*my bedroom!*—and saw this homeless dude, she freaked."

"You know," Barley tells him, "if only one person tells a story about someone being belligerent then I don't pay much attention. But I've had three independently thinking people tell me about your temper."

Skizzy laughs at the ceiling. "I'll bet you have. Just look at me! I'm a dude in a muumuu that smells like whiskey. When I was a kid my stepdad, Bobby McEvil #2, lost his favorite *Anal Betty* magazine. Who do you think he beat the hell out of? Of course, when he finally found it in the crack between the bed and the wall, I told him *See, I told you it wasn't me* so he smacked me in the face with a fishing pole. Ha!"

Skizzy picks up a glass and looks at Barley through the beer. His left eye is visible through the glass. It is yellow. "Remember: God is watching," he says. "Every minute."

Barley looks at the bar clock. He didn't want to come here in the first place but Skizzy called for a ride. He's always calling for something. Today he offered to buy Barley a beer in exchange for a ride home, and Barley figured a beer is worth listening to Skizzy's delusions.

"Well," Skizzy says, "it's mighty cold tonight." He watches the ceiling fan circulate the warm air down to the floor. "Yeah. Mighty cold."

"Well, you're staying with Abbi. She has a heater."

"Abbi? Ha! She's usually not even there. And she didn't give me a key."

"Now I understand. You need a place to stay. But you didn't want to ask me for a place when you called—you were afraid I'd refuse. So you said you needed a ride. Then you bought a couple of beers, and now I'm stuck with you. You're my problem."

"Man, I'm just a human being looking for a floor to catch my dreams and a heater to keep me alive."

"I'll take you to Abbi's house. Maybe she's there."

Abbi's house is ghostly. Barley and Skizzy sit in the car and stare.

Finally Skizzy breaks the silence, his voice as small as a puppy's: "Well, I can just wait here in the cold. She'll get home eventually. Don't worry about me. I'm a survivor. Did I tell you I fell off a moving train? Pinched my right nut between the cars. Don't worry, though. My pecker still works."

"Skizzy, a lot of people are afraid of you. You've never made me fear for my safety. But I still don't want you knowing where I live. I get the feeling you'd end up camping in my yard and screaming at random people in the middle of the night."

"I've done it before. Ha!"

"Let me drive you to the shelter."

"The shelter? Man, they hate me there. The guy who runs the place, Rodrigo Bunnyfucker, grabbed me by the coat and told me to get out. I told him, 'Hey, there's no need to get violent. Just let me go, and I'll walk out peacefully.' But he didn't. He kept grabbing me and shoving me toward the door. I told him, 'Look, if you don't stop shoving me, I'm gonna hit you with my walking stick,' and he didn't believe me! He just kept pushing. So I whacked him! Right over the head! Yeah!"

"Yeah."

More silence. A snowflake drifts onto the windshield and melts. "I don't even need a pillow. I can sleep on anything."

"You're not staying at my house."

"Fine." Skizzy lifts his chin. "I never stay where I'm not welcome." He opens the car door and climbs out. A mass of winter rushes into the car.

Skizzy ruffles through his backpack and pulls out a crinkled twenty-dollar bill. He flings the bill onto the passenger seat. "Here's for your troubles."

"Skizzy, I can't take money from you."

"No, I insist. I fucking insist."

"Then put it toward a motel room. I'll pay the rest."

"I ain't wasting my money on a motel. I'd rather give it to someone who needs it. And if you're too desperate to let a man sleep on your floor on a cold night, then you need twenty dollars worse than I do."

"Fine."

"Just remember," he says, "you'll need help someday. And the Lord will remember what you did tonight. But that's fine with me. I don't want to be a bother to anybody ever." The door slams shut.

A police cruiser is parked on the same block. Skizzy flails his cloak all the way to the cruiser, then bangs his walking stick on its roof. Two cops emerge from the cruiser and help Skizzy disappear from view, if only for a night.

Jesus Jill
Snares the Soul

Deanna Hendrix floats her prayers in a cloud of incense. Her chants are directed toward a hippie-softened version of the Hebrew city-destroyer Yahweh (or, to the Gentiles: God). Deanna's daughter Stella, on the other hand, sees a much broader definition of deity. Stella believes in "every god ever fabricated, Mom. Even yours."

Stella's unorthodoxy has made her a target of conversation at school, particularly among students who wouldn't dare talk to her for fear of eternal damnation. For instance, Kiki Meyers enjoys speculating about the temperature of the fire that will cook Stella's organs in the Afterlife. Will Satan slow-roast her like a turkey or scorch her like bacon? God only knows. And also Satan.

Kiki's more compassionate partner-in-faith Jill Boudreaux repeatedly asks God for assistance in winning Stella's soul. God's answer is always the same: *Talk to her, Jill. Make friends with her. Show interest in her hobbies. Wait for the right time and then invite her to church. Have faith—the Truth is yours to share.*

Jill has repeatedly tried to approach Stella but Stella can

be an intimidating presence. Today Jill sees Stella walking in the hallway, staring at the far wall as though she were seducing a priest. Jill takes steps to intercept, asserting herself through the oncoming foot traffic, and manages to get close enough to whisper a squeaky "Hi."

Stella, not slowing her stride, looks directly at Jill for an instant. Jill finds herself overcome by something that resembles an asthma attack: shallow breath, tense, gasp, tense—*my God,* Jill thinks. *Stella Hendrix, the girl my Bible Study calls Satan's Spine, is locked eye-to-eye with me.* Jill makes a panicked left turn toward the wall of lockers and squats behind Stella's plane of vision. She leans into a locker and collects her breath.

Satan's Spine loves nothing more than talking about religion. Dennis Carpenter, who smells like day-old pizza, now sits on Stella's unmade bed trying to make sense of the Book of Matthew, specifically the verse that says "If thy right eye offend thee, pluck it out."

"Wow," says Dennis. "That's harsh. Whatever the cause of your sin, *pluck it out*, even if it's a part of your own body."

Dennis's right eye doesn't offend him much, nor does his left eye. The organ that offends him the most, the apparent root of his overwhelming sin, is halfway between his eyes and the ground. It flinched the first time Stella laughed in his presence. It inflated, if only slightly, a few minutes ago when he followed her into her room, and again when he saw the black cotton panties topping the pheromone-scented pile of clothes next to the bed, now teasing his bare and dangling ankle. The scant hair on his calf is reaching out from his skin to catch stray electrons from the laundry mound. Each captured electron flows up Dennis's leg to his most offensive organ, which Jesus demands be plucked out. Dennis decides he needs a new religion.

"Great!" Stella says. "I love religions. Let's make one."

Dennis looks at her like she might be a spy for the Neo-McCarthyites. "Make one?"

"Yes! A new religion. We'll call it Stella-Dennis-ism. Or Stennicism. Yes! Our followers will be called Stennics."

Dennis may have had a lover's spat with Christianity, but he isn't ready to risk God's revenge by ending the relationship. What if, by even playfully creating a new religion, Dennis would condemn himself to having his bones smashed, re-cemented, torched, hosed with acid, run through a meat grinder, and reconstructed like clay by demon kindergarteners, only to be torched again, day after day, trillion years after trillion years, so far into the future that he won't even remember his fleeting decades on Earth, and he certainly won't remember why he's being punished—torture for eternity! What if!

On the other hand, creating a religion sounds like fun. And like his devout Christian friends, Dennis is willing to risk eternity for a little fun.

Stella and Dennis throw wads of paper at each other as they build and rebuild the gods of their new religion. One thing they agree on: if they're going to make holy thrones then they might as well sit in them. Stella and Dennis ask one another what kind of deities they would like to be. Omnipotent? Certainly.

Loving? Too much trouble. After all, there are billions of people on Earth, to say nothing for the octopi, moss, bacteria, and things humans haven't discovered. Besides, Earth is probably not the only living planet in the Universe. There must be billions of living planets. How can two deities coordinate the lives of so many beings? And why would they want to? Stella and Dennis may be omnipotent but they're not bureaucrats. Let the beings live and die as their genes dictate.

THE STENNIC MANIFESTO

I. Deities.

The Stennics recognize the Creators, one God and one Goddess. They are not your Father and Mother. They will not grant you an afterlife. When you die, you're dead.

Stella lights some incense. They throw their prejudices into a system of beliefs.

II. Beliefs.

The creed of the Stennics contains four absolutes, namely that:

1. The law is written and enforced by people who consider themselves exempt from it.

2. Authority is powered by oppression.

3. The oppressed have the power to unite, focus, and overthrow authority.

4. When the oppressed decide to overthrow and thereby become authority, the cycle begins anew.

Dennis concedes that oppression and overthrow are common themes in human history. "But," he says, "historical patterns aren't enough to make a *bona fide* religion. A religion needs a system of morals."

Stella counters that morals are nothing but a way to enforce authority. The Stennic Manifesto is designed to expose authority, not to enforce it. "Besides," she says, "I don't have any morals."

"No morals at all?" Dennis asks.

"None."

Dennis: "Have you ever molested an infant?"

Stella assures Dennis that she has never molested an infant.

Dennis asks, "If you really have no morals, then why haven't you molested an infant?"

Stella replies, "Because I've never felt the desire."

Dennis gulps.

III. Morals.

> The creed of the Stennics is not moral in any
> sense. Rather, the creed is simply true. If you
> live by its wisdom then you are more likely to
> survive the next revolution.

After the rambling is set to paper, Stella and Dennis watch one another across the flame on the lanky candle that balances precariously on the bed. Silence flickers. Their manifesto is complete, and Dennis has eleven minutes until his curfew. The return trip takes nine minutes, leaving them two full minutes for a goodbye hug.

As Dennis pulls out of the driveway, Satan's Spine realizes that the copy store will be open for another hour. She can make hundreds of manifestos by morning. Her exhaustion lifts.

As a new scholastic day begins, a new religion undergoes its first day of persecution. At midnight last night, Day Zero on the Stennic calendar, the creative Goddess gained access to Benjamin High School through the Friends of the Devilhorns Annex and slipped Stennic Manifestos through hundreds of locker vents.

The manifestos are now circulating among the students. Teachers' reactions vary widely.

Mr. D'Ott, the art teacher, is joyous that such non-apathetic self-expression is asserting itself among the students.

Miss Prattle, the English teacher, is biting her thumb because she fears being accused of inciting a revolt. She paces her classroom trying to lecture on Whitman but her mind keeps coming back to *I shouldn't have shown* Dead Poets Society. *This will all come down on my shoulders.*

Coach Cobb, who somehow teaches Algebra II, reminds his class that tampering with another student's locker is grounds for expulsion and that breaking and entering into the school is a crime. Therefore enough extra credit to win an A in the class will be awarded for information leading to the expulsion and arrest of the godless perpetrator.

As Coach Cobb issues the proclamation, Dennis becomes suddenly aware of himself. He tries not to look guilty. His mouth is a sponge.

Sitting next to Dennis, Jill Boudreaux smiles like she knows a secret. She is using a yellow highlighter to make large letters on a piece of notebook paper. Dennis strains to see what she's writing. When Jill is finished, she traces the letters with orange, then with green, and finally with blue. Her smile widens as she folds the paper in half.

Jill leans toward Dennis as though she wants to include him in something. She whispers into his ear with un-Jill-like sensuality, "I know who the godless perpetrator is."

Dennis loses his breath. It takes real effort to pronounce: "Who?"

Jill licks her molars and unfolds the paper.

Dennis: "How do you know?"

The conversation is interrupted by Coach Cobb, who

insists that Dennis and Jill should smooch after school, not during Algebra II. Twenty kids chuckle, and suddenly the whole universe is looking at Jill and Dennis. Jill doesn't seem to mind. Dennis definitely does.

Stella walks the lunchtime hall of the art wing, high on the realization that her prank has created a greater stir than she anticipated. Five girls from social cliques ranging from Glitter Punk to Cheerleader have shown copies of the manifesto to Stella. The girls chose their words carefully, as though they hoped Stella would let slip a confession.

Stella sees Dennis and greets him with a smile that shows off her gums.

Dennis is not smiling. His lips get close enough to spew moisture as he hisses, "We need to talk."

Stella reconsiders her ecstasy. "As you like it," she says.

They duck into the drama room and hide behind the stage curtains.

Dennis: "You didn't tell me you were going to distribute the manifesto."

Stella: "The opportunity presented itself."

"We could both be expelled, Stella. You could go to jail."

"Not if we both keep our mouths shut."

"It's too late. Jill Boudreaux knows you did it."

"Jill who?"

"Jill Boudreaux." Dennis searches for an appropriate description, and comes up with, "The girl who writes love notes to Jesus."

Stella laughs loudly enough to be heard in the hallway. "So Jesus Jill is convinced that I'm the Stennic Goddess? Since there's no way she could know by earthly means, she must've heard it from Jesus himself. Wow!"

Dennis isn't amused.

Stella softens her tone. "Dennis, sometimes I forget that you still believe—or at least a part of you believes—that there's a giant camera in the sky that records your every action. That you can never get away with anything because some god—or some mother, or some teacher—will always find out what you've done. Well, you're wrong, Dennis. You won't go to hell for creating the manifesto, and you won't get expelled from school. Not if we both keep our mouths shut."

Stella puts her hand on Dennis's shoulder. "I've actually heard people questioning their beliefs today. We did a good thing, Dennis. And best of all, we'll get away with it—if we both keep our mouths shut."

Dennis is beginning to feel better. Stella has a point: unless Jill actually saw Stella sneaking into the school last night, there is no way Jill could know who distributed the manifesto. Dennis takes his first full breath since he arrived at school. Things may work out after all.

Dennis slips out from behind the stage curtain with a renewed sense of confidence. The confidence is brief, however, lasting exactly long enough for Dennis and Stella, each in their turn, to notice the giant eavesdropping ear of Jesus Jill Boudreaux, who is smiling in the drama room doorway. Dennis and Stella freeze.

"You're right, Stella," Jill says. "Jesus did tell me you were the godless perpetrator. But nobody listens to Jesus anymore, so the information was useless. Praise God, I've now heard it from the source."

Stella: "What do you want, Jill?"

Jill's eyes shine with victory.

Stella looks around the room. The walls are made of the kind of concrete blocks that are normally used in house foundations. The room is lit by obscene strips of fluorescence. The top of the room is barely six feet from the floor. A human-sized wooden cross dominates the front wall, stretching from floor to ceiling in an apparent attempt to burst through the roof.

The room contains a circle of metal chairs. Occupying the chairs are seven teenagers who are amazed by Stella's presence. They don't often get newcomers here, certainly not many with the reputation of Satan's Spine.

To Stella's left sits Dennis, looking every bit as uncomfortable as Stella.

To her right sits Jesus Jill Boudreaux, whose forehead is shining to the sky. Jill seems to be having a silent, very personal conversation with God.

In the room's only cushioned chair, Kiki Meyers is leading a discussion on why Catholics aren't really Christians. Stella holds back. *Your life is a sham,* she wants to say. *You're letting this church dictate your thoughts, your politics and your prejudice— and for what? The ecstasy of prayer? The certainty of being right?*

The comfort of groupthink? You don't need a church for that! Stella settles in her chair. She reminds herself that the people in this room don't want to have a conversation with her. They may think they do, but they really don't.

Fresh off the line with God, Jill opens her eyes and gazes at Stella like a hunter might gaze at the trophy-head of an elephant. Jill whispers, "I'm so glad you came to church, Stella. You may not like it now, but I promise: you'll thank me in the Afterlife."

Satan's Spine curses with her eyes but keeps her mouth shut.

Carney's Stellar Banana Trip

On a wet April Saturday, meat tycoon Clemens Bison returned to his birthtown of Benjamin to unveil the statue of his likeness in the town square. During the ceremony, a funny-looking young man named Carney Banks snagged the wallet of Clemens and his forty-year-old son Jim, the town's only billionaires. Carney's cash winnings totaled $221, much less than he'd anticipated, but still his highest score ever.

The Bison wallets, complete with canceled credit cards and photos of extremely wealthy infants, lie in the little treasure chest that Carney stole from the discount superstore the following day.

Now, as he walks along the storefront row across the street from Town Square, Carney notices what seems to be a very limber mannequin behind the shop window of the incense store. She is lying on a couch with one bare leg outstretched and the other forming a triangle between her thigh, her calf, and the cushion. The curls dangling from the mannequin's head have fallen over her face as she looks downward at a book.

After a moment, the mannequin breaks her stillness and

looks up at Carney. Carney jolts. It takes a wobbling second for the plastic face to mold itself into the flesh of Stella Hendrix, the girl at school who likes to tell people that, given the choice, she'd rather go to Hell than Heaven because Heaven has too many Baptists. When she recognizes Carney, a demonic smile overwrites her face before she rolls over the back of the couch and lands in a walking position on her way to the shop's front door.

Four seconds later, Stella is standing in front of Carney on the sidewalk. "Hey," she says, looking directly into his eyes and forcing her way into his psyche, "I know you. You stole Clemens Bison's wallet."

Carney leans backward as though flinching from a campfire that has just been doused with gasoline. How could she possibly know that? Carney didn't tell anyone except his smoking buddy Winston, and Winston wouldn't tell anyone. Not Winston. No way.

"No, I didn't," says Carney, and gulps.

"I heard that you did," says Stella. "And I believe it. I think you're skilled enough to pull it off."

Carney allows himself the conceit of analyzing the skill it took to rip off two billionaires while surrounded by spectators and cops. Most people wouldn't appreciate that skill, but Stella does. *But, Carney thinks, don't let yourself be flattered by this woman. Concentrate! She could be dangerous if she really knows.* He tries to straighten his mind enough to respond with a tactical question, something brilliant enough to find out exactly what she knows without admitting guilt, but his tongue can only form the words "Who told you?"

Her eyes are snakes. She answers, "Jesus told me."

In a burst of inspiration, as though someone else were controlling his tongue, Carney says, "Jesus doesn't talk to you." *Good*, Carney coaches himself. *Keep it simple.* He has had difficulty concentrating all day, and the present moment is no exception. Carney continues, "You don't believe in Jesus."

Her eyes hover next to his face. He wants her to back up and keep backing up until she disappears tail-first around a corner. But she doesn't. Instead she says, "Jesus and I talk all the time. We drink wine together on Sundays."

Drinking with Jesus reminds Carney of a guy he met last night. The guy looked very much like Jesus. Carney bought ten hits of acid from him. Carney had planned on being frugal and taking two or three hits at a time, but this morning he decided— what the hell—to take six. Although the peak effects wore off by the time school ended, Stella's presence is causing Carney's chemical breakfast to flood his psyche once more.

Stella's fingers wrap around Carney's wrist like a handcuff. She pulls him into her mother's incense store, across an oppressive cloud of sandalwood, through a back door and up some stairs.

Carney finds himself in a small living room with a retro-green love seat and three beanbags. The furniture contrasts itself in a kindergarten color scheme. Stella sits on one bag and Carney finds himself plopped on the other two. The bags shift underneath him like a fishing boat. Both of her hands are now cuffing his wrists, stabilizing his balance. She looks directly into him and reads the history of theft in his eyes.

Stella: "How did you do it?"

He watches her lean forward in slow motion. Her face settles close enough to spark a tiny lightning arc on his cheek. Her breath cooks his ear.

Stella whispers, "Show me how to steal."

For a vibrating second Carney and Stella become one. Carney then pulls his right hand from under his leg. His two cigarette fingers point to the ceiling. Held between the fingers, displayed like a rigid flag, is a neatly folded twenty-dollar bill. He offers her the money.

She studies the bill, trying to decide why he wants to give it to her.

"Here," Carney says, watching her face melt into a tender state of confusion. "This is yours. I found it in the flat space between your zipper and your skin."

Stella touches her money spot and realizes that he's right.

―――――――――――

Carney leads Stella through the tall rectangular aisles of the discount superstore. He feels himself in an unfamiliar role: he is playing teacher. "When you commit to stealing," he instructs, "you are declaring war. Humanity's most revered strategist, Sun Tsu, said that war is about deceit.

"If you had money, you could take what you want by diplomatic trade. But you have no funds, no leverage, so diplomacy is useless." Carney points his eyes to the black globes hiding cameras on the ceiling. "The enemy outnumbers you 100 to 1, and his spies are all over the sky. Also, the store has an alliance with a very powerful army: the police force. Therefore, doing battle—that is, threatening the enemy with violence—is unwise."

The thief and his protégé stop in the aisle of digital cameras. Stella uses her fingers to examine a combination photo and movie camera.

Carney compliments her choice. "You hold a high density of wealth in your hands. The most gain for the least effort."

Stella walks into an awkward corner of the aisle. She's not quite out of the ceiling globe's hemisphere of vision, but her back is between the globe and the loot. She cradles the prize into her purse.

"You look like a thief," Carney says. Stella stops, apparently awaiting instructions. Carney tells her, "Bring the item back into view. Let the world see it."

Stella stands up slowly, letting the camera sit in her hands.

"Good," he says. "Now, what do you hold in your hands?"

Stella: "A camera."

Carney: "Bananas."

Stella looks confused. "Bananas?"

Carney: "We came here to buy bananas. Nothing more. Your heart rate should be at banana-level. You're an actress. You're holding a prop. The prop is bananas. Look at the bananas in your hand."

Stella looks at the camera and tries to envision bananas.

Carney: "Let's go pay for the bananas."

Pay? For the first time Stella doubts the ability of her teacher. How are they going to get the camera out the front door? She can pretend to carry bananas, but the cashier will see the camera. Maybe they'll take the camera to the self-pay machine, but the old woman at the front door will see the camera. Stella suspects that Carney's hallucinogens might be a disadvantage. "Look, Carney," she says, "I don't—"

"Bananas."

When the pair reach the self-check aisle, Stella feels like every globe on the ceiling is watching her. Carney takes the camera from her. Rather than scanning the barcode, he sets the camera on the scale as though it were a piece of produce. He then types a PLU number into the keypad. The screen displays the word "Bananas." Carney pulls some bills from his pocket and feeds the machine a dollar amount worth the camera's weight in bananas.

When they exit the store, the alarm sounds. The old woman walks toward them. Carney rolls his eyes and talks to the old woman as though she were a friend. "I hate it when that happens."

"Yeah," the woman replies. "Sometimes the security bar doesn't deactivate right. Let me see your receipt."

Carney hands the old woman the receipt. She marks it with a colored marker. "Thank you," she tells him.

"Thank you very much," Carney says.

Holy shit, Stella thinks. *He did it!* The pair take steps into the parking lot, for the first time allowing themselves to feel the adrenaline high of victory. Their smiles are about to turn into laughter when they hear the old smoker's voice behind them: "Wait a minute. Come back here!"

The old woman's footsteps click behind them. Younger, quicker pursuers are sure to follow. Carney quickens his pace and quotes more wisdom from Sun Tsu: "When you're outnumbered, run away if you can."

Stella follows Carney's sprint across the parking lot. Definitely more pursuers now. A small troop of discount superstore associates. Carney and Stella run for the woods— there's a creek in there. Jolting steps, the world flies by in colors. Stella hasn't felt this alive in years. She's an animal in survival mode. Stella and Carney versus the universe. Run!

There's a car parked in the darkest corner of the lot. Stella normally wouldn't notice it, but the car is unusual for this part of the state. It is a Bentley. Worth more than a small mansion.

Carney takes a sudden turn toward the Bentley. "Follow me!"

Stella is horrified and confused. *The woods are right there*, she thinks. *We could make it!* She looks at the woods—she's certain that if she stayed the course then she could cross the creek before the pursuers caught her. The pursuers would probably give up rather than splash through the water. She's certain of that. Well, not completely certain. Not certain at all. *Damn you, Carney!*

Not because of logic, but rather from a groupthink sense of loyalty, Stella follows Carney toward the Bentley. As they approach the car, Stella's ears pick up the sound of car doors simultaneously locking. *Someone's in the car!*

The pursuing army of discount employees is hurling demands for the thieves to stop.

Carney bangs on the driver's side window. He shouts to the driver, "We need a ride!"

The engine starts. Stella sees the old man in the driver seat. The terror in his eyes. The realization hits her: *We're carjacking him.*

Stella feels the situation ballooning beyond her control. Carney is repeating his demand for a ride. A much younger man in the passenger seat is squirming, perhaps reaching for a weapon. Stella does not want to be standing still. The employees are a few dozen yards away. The woods are within reach. The young man in the passenger seat—what is he doing?

The passenger is zipping his pants.

The engine drops into reverse. Carney holds the camera to the windshield and snaps a picture. Blinding flash. Then another. As the car begins its backward trajectory, screeching its wheels and startling the pursuers for a second, Stella finally recognizes the driver. *Of course! Who else in Benjamin can afford a Bentley?*

Carney rounds the car, positions himself directly in front of the bumper, snaps another picture and yells, "Clemens Bison! Homosexual liaison! I have pictures!"

The car stops. The young passenger is in hysterics, urging Clemens Bison to "Go, go, drive, damn you, old man, go!"

Carney repeats his command: "Give us a ride!"

The employees begin their descent toward the car. Suddenly the creek seems fifty miles away. Clemens Bison is hesitating. The passenger is squealing. Carney is holding the camera outward like a police badge. The flash bulb blinds everyone again. The employees' footfalls echo from surrounding angles.

Within a span of time that feels like a movie frame, Stella finds herself crunched next to Carney in the back seat of the Bentley. The car is swerving in desperate maneuvers that send the discount employees scattering.

As the car makes a shrill turn onto Bison Avenue, a mammalian screech flies from the young passenger's throat. He turns his shoulder toward the back seat and uses his hand as a weapon against Carney and Stella. The passenger seat protects his body and face as he claws Carney's skin and grabs Stella's hair. The car is compact; Stella can barely unfold her leg enough to kick the attacker. Her calf gets caught in the young man's clutches. He grips his teeth on the meat of Stella's leg, breaking her skin and branding his bloody dental records onto her calf.

Stella can't see the front windshield, but judging from the G-forces sloshing her in random directions, Stella knows that the car is occupying at least two lanes. Clemens Bison yells "Stop it!" With his right hand he pushes the passenger's face away from Stella's leg. With his left hand he avoids a head-on collision. "Stop it! All of you!"

Clemens turns the Bentley onto a dimly lit road. The car is filled with heavy breathing. The old man parks. The young man is glaring from Carney to Stella and back again like a leashed dog waiting to be given enough slack to attack. The old man turns the rearview mirror until his eyes meet Carney's. In a thick, boss-like voice, Clemens says, "Give me the camera."

Carney stares back at the wrinkled eyes in the mirror. He retorts, "Give me a thousand dollars."

"How dare you!"

Silence turns cold. Clemens reassures himself with a long breath. "I already gave you a ride. And I could give you another ride: directly to jail. I own the police."

Carney: "I own the camera."

The young passenger asserts himself: "Give him the fucking camera!" Clemens silences him with a quick but unmistakable sidelong glare.

Stella wants the situation to end. She gropes the door in search of the unlocking mechanism. Carney places his hand on her leg. He fails to calm her.

The old man's face softens. He seems almost grandfatherly. "I like you, son. Your instincts are sharp and you're not afraid to use them. You're also ruthless. You'll be a billionaire if you can stay out of prison. Your problem is that you're not ambitious enough. You just risked becoming a slave to the prison system for less money than I spent on my date tonight. Breaking the law is a commoner's game. I don't break the law. I write the law to my advantage. I use it to take what I want. You can too, if you'll let me show you how. What's your name, Son?"

Stella finds the unlocking mechanism and releases herself from the car. Within seconds she is making fast, heavy footsteps through the woods.

———————————

As the shock wears thin, the pain in Stella's calf makes itself real. Her knees drop her, sobbing, onto the leafy floor of a dark wood on the edge of Bison Creek Park. Sobbing!

She can't remember the last time she sobbed. Somewhere in the darkness, twigs are snapping. Leaves are mashing under footsteps. Someone is looking for her.

Stella's survival sense comes back online. She slows her breathing and tries to be inaudible. Too late. Feet appear in front of her. Tattered tennis shoes.

"Hey," says Carney.

Stella refuses to look up. "Go away."

Carney stays where he is. "You don't have any right to be mad at me. I did what you asked. I showed you how to steal."

"I never asked you to carjack anyone."

"We didn't carjack just anyone," Carney said. "We carjacked Clemens Bison."

"It doesn't matter. You can't live your life that way, stealing from people—or else you'll end up just like Clemens Bison, hiding from your secrets until you die."

Carney stops himself from unleashing a violent reaction onto a tree. "Don't tell me what I can't do." Carney looks up into the blackness for a moment, wishing the crickets could chirp loudly enough to overcome the silence. Finally he decides to make amends. "We should get you cleaned up."

Stella's curiosity overtakes her. "Did you get the bananas?"

Carney lets out the first breath of a laugh. "No."

"Did you get any money?"

"No," he says, "but I did get a story. Before I smashed the camera, I looked into the eyes of Clemens Bison, the wealthiest man I've ever met, and told him that on April 12 his wallet disappeared on Town Square and I'm the son of a bitch that took it. I watched his eyes reveal their devil nature. Then I escaped."

Stella looks up. "But why didn't you get any loot? You had leverage. You could've gotten what you wanted."

"What I wanted," Carney says, "ran into the woods."

Stella lets the statement settle. She considers a possible future as the girlfriend of Carney Banks. There will be no puppy love. He will not bow to her in irritating worship. Instead he will love her with burning desperation. He will touch her like only the introverted can. He will lie to her. At least once he will call her from jail. He is a firecracker in a package of firecrackers.

So her choice is this: either live a few months of raw insanity with Carney Banks, or hang around the incense store reading more of her mother's books on the healing power of crystals.

Stella wraps her fingers around Carney's wrist. She pulls him down into the bed of leaves.

Facebook Poltergeist

Skizzy doesn't want much. He is accustomed to having very little. His desires are limited to the present day, and all he wants today is to star in his own meme and post it on Facebook.

He imagines the meme in brighter colors than are generally believed to exist. The scene is a screen-sized photo of Skizzy with his week-old beard, his torso and midsection covered with a crudely stitched cotton rectangle. He's holding his walking stick in the air with viral words like:

FIGHTS FOR GAY MARRIAGE

CALLS HIS MOTHER A FAG

or, better yet,

VEGETERIAN

CANNIBAL

which would imply that Skizzy is a plant.

Skizzy has always wanted to be a plant, specifically a Redwood tree. Honorable creature, the Redwood. It claims a plot of ground and refuses to leave for 2,000 years. The Redwood calmly observes the empires that rise and fall around it. Skizzy would like to be like that. Not aggressive, exactly, though he wouldn't mind if his bark evolved a welder's arc that shot lightning at lumberjacks. Purely defensive. He claimed this land, after all, and he's not moving. Not for anyone. Not ever.

Skizzy's walking stick is made of Redwood, at least according to Dreadlock Dave, the wannabe homeless kid who tried to sell it to him. Imagine! Walking around a perfectly peaceful music festival hawking walking sticks with a "Genuine Redwood" label. There were only two possible interpretations: either Dreadlock Dave had paid wholesale money for the holy corpse of a being with a 2,000-year lifespan, or else Dreadlock Dave was a lying shitfucker. In either case, he needed a good beating.

Redwood walking sticks, sale sale sale. "I have to sell them quick," said Dreadlock Dace, "because my grandmother needs a new hip. I can't believe I'm selling them this cheap." Skizzy asked to examine one.

Skizzy's plan was simple: complete his Dave-beating and then ceremoniously give the stick to the nearest campfire for a proper Redwood cremation. He maintained his plan until his hand closed around the walking stick. Then, in the time it took for the nerve endings in his palm to communicate with his brain, Skizzy's life changed.

The stick was a telepath. It was female despite its lack of

genitalia. "Yes," she said. "I really am made of Redwood. I'm just a splinter of my former self, but it takes more than a giant chainsaw to kill me. I've been waiting for you, Skizzy. Take me with you."

The first part of Skizzy's plan remained intact. He whacked Dreadlock Dave in the knee, possibly breaking it, and left the neo-Hippie on the ground to scream like the privileged infant he really was. But the second part of Skizzy's plan was cancelled. There would be no cremation for this Redwood. Cremation is for the dead.

Now all Skizzy wants is a Facebook meme.

WHACKS REDWOOD TREEKILLER

CARRIES REDWOOD WALKING STICK

First step: find a camera.

Everyone has a camera nowadays. Skizzy, minding his own business on a busy sidewalk, happens to be surrounded by everyone. He sees a nice-looking woman who looks economically connected enough to have a camera-ridden cell phone. "Excuse me!" he says. "Yeah, you. Honey. I need you to—" but the woman just gives him the terror eyes and walks quickly past.

Dammit. Women are easily spooked nowadays. Too many frat boys slipping them drugs. Assholes. Fine—Skizzy will ask a man instead. Ooh! Here's a man with a beer belly. Looks like he has probably pissed on a party lawn or two. Skizzy's kind of guy. "Excuse me! Yeah, you. Buddy. I need you to—" but the man just mumbles something about not carrying cash. Skizzy follows him. "I didn't ask for money, you bourgeois sack of turd meat!"

Everyone is scared of Skizzy today. Clearly God is angry with him.

God speaks to Skizzy every minute, especially through the little human interactions he endures in public, some verbal, but most involving subtle changes in eye contact or body language. Some days God allows the world to be calm around him—that is, on some days people barely notice him. But today the people are walking wide paths around him. Today God is irritated.

Why is God angry? Possibly because Skizzy stopped taking his meds. He can't afford them anyway, and even if he could, why would he want to take them? He would just end up like the bourgeois sack of turd meat, too connected to the money circulation machine to stop and take a picture for a live human stranger. *Go home, beer belly! Interact with the television. It'll be a lot safer, except for the whole brainwashing thing.*

BELIEVES CAMERAS STEAL YOUR SOUL

BEGS YOU TO TAKE HIS PICTURE

Much like a Redwood, Skizzy's soul is old and massive. He can afford to lose a splinter to a Facebook meme. He needs to find a camera. He needs to make peace with God so the people will be receptive.

Standing still in a moving crowd, Skizzy lifts Redwood to

the sky. "All right, God! You win! I am a small, selfish, hairless ape. I spend my days trying to eat, fuck and get high. There. I admitted it. I am dogshit sticking to the sole of a Republican's shoe. I need you. I'll say Hail Marys until the sun comes up. Now may I please have a fucking camera?"

Then comes the Voice: "Skizzy?"

Skizzy stumbles backward. He is startled. God talks to Skizzy every minute, but rarely does He use His Own Voice to call Skizzy by name. "Skizzy," the Voice says again, "what are you doing?"

Oh! That isn't the Voice of God. That's a human voice. The voice is to his left. There it is again: "Calm down, brother. You're surrounded by love."

Jesus. The voice belongs to Barley Hopps. Good to smoke with and bum cheap beer. But damn, Barley can be irritating. Love this, love that, love everybody. Barley loves the thug who left him bloody on the sidewalk for thirty bucks. He loves the cop who shredded his couch and dragged him to jail for the crime of selling a plant. Skizzy doesn't approve of universal love because love is too precious to be wasted on muggers and cops. But poor enlightened Barley loves everyone.

Irritating though he is, Barley has a job and a phone. Most likely he has a camera. "Barley! I need you to take a picture of me."

Snap. Picture taken. Barley says, "Is that what you need, brother?"

Skizzy: "You're not my brother. I sucked my brother's dick from my fifth birthday to the day he went to prison. So unless you're offering—"

"I'm not offering, Skizzy."

"Good. Then don't call me brother. Yeah. I need you to give me that picture."

"I'll email it to you."

"Great. Now I need to use your computer."

"Sorry, Skizzy. I'm on my way to work. If you need a computer, you should go to the library."

"I can't go to the library. That place scares the soul out of me. It has poltergeists. They throw books. Over and over again those damned poltergeists dropped *Harlequin Romances* on my head. Well, one day I'd had enough. I caught one of the books and threw it on the floor. I beat that *Romance* until it was pile of scrap. I didn't know whether it would work—I just knew I had to do it—and guess what! I killed the poltergeist. Of course its friends are still infesting the place. But I proved: we can beat them!

"But do you know what the shitfucking librarian did? She called the cops. The cops! After I killed a poltergeist in her library. So she won't let me in her library anymore. She won't let me make a Facebook meme. She won't even let me check my messages."

DOESN'T BELIEVE IN GHOSTS

KILLED A FUCKING POLTERGEIST

Barley puts his arms around Skizzy in what is supposed

52

to be a soothing, if unsolicited, hug. Skizzy's instinctive urge is to stick the shiny end of his switchblade into Barley's balls, but instead he chooses to wait out the assault. Deep inside Skizzy's personal perimeter, Barley whispers, "You catch more vinegar with flies in honey."

Skizzy doesn't know what to make of that statement. When Barley breaks the hug and makes his way toward whatever jerk is keeping him employed, Skizzy decides to interpret the statement in the same way he interprets everything that doesn't make sense: the statement is a gift from God.

God is telling Skizzy to be nice to the librarian. Don't antagonize her. Just sneak by her and smile.

Skizzy makes himself invisible and walks Redwood to the realm of poltergeists and librarians.

Facebook, prepare to be memed.

"Attention, library staff. We have a Code Maybe. Repeat: Code Maybe."

There is no Code Maybe in the library handbook. Code Maybe was introduced informally after a crazy man beat a library book in the romance aisle. Code Maybe tells the staff that Skizzy is back.

Librarian Grayson Mandy intercepts Skizzy in the lobby and blocks his path with a wide smile. "Hello, Skizzy."

"Outta my way, you perfumed—" Skizzy stops for a moment. He reflects on the message from God, and then assumes a submissive posture. "I would like to use a computer, please."

"Certainly you may use a computer, Skizzy. But you must leave your staff at the front desk."

"Seriously? I ain't leavin' Redwood with nobody! You're liable to grind her up for pulp. I know how you librarians love paper."

"No one will harm your staff, Skizzy. You have my word."

"But Redwood is a gift from God! She looks after me. Protects me. Keeps me outta trouble. I can't give her up."

"You can't bring your staff into the library, Skizzy."

"Damn you, woman!" Skizzy considers his options. Submission didn't work, and aggression gets no respect in the library. How about flirtation? That sometimes works. He gives it a shot: "You know, you're pretty tall for a girl. Built like a man. I like that. Do you like penises? Mine's not the biggest in the world, but I know how to—"

The librarian has inhaled all the air in the room. "Please leave the library."

"I just need a computer."

She gives the air back. "Goodbye, Skizzy."

It's obvious now that the perfumed librarian is in league with the poltergeists. She is their protector. Skizzy doesn't know whether she has some symbiotic relationship with them or just feels maternal. Her motivation doesn't matter. She has given the poltergeists free reign in the library.

The situation must be remedied.

"You can't burn down the library, bro."

Damn it. Skizzy should have known that Barley would care more about Earthly morality and legal consequences than about a *bona fide* preternatural threat. Sure, a fire would cause millions of dollars in damage and destroy unique artifacts of local history. And sure, Skizzy and Barley would have to bite a few faces in prison. But at least the schoolchildren wouldn't be pelted by poltergeists. Maybe Skizzy can make Barley understand. He explains, "You can't kill a coven of otherworldly beings one by one. You have to attack them in their lair. You have to come at them from the sun."

Barley looks into his beer. Skizzy decides that it's useless to talk strategy with a pacifist. He stomps Redwood on the bar floor, drawing a glare from the tattooed barkeep. "I don't need your permission, *bro*. I just need your help."

"All I'm asking is that you take your meds for a couple of days and then think it over."

"When I take my meds I lose my clarity, you cop-loving masochist."

"Alright, Skizzy. I'll help you get rid of the poltergeists. But you don't really need to burn down the whole library, do you?"

"Just the *Harlequin Romances*."

"That would increase the literary quality of the library."

"No shit."

Barley offers a plan. Although the romance section contains several dozen books, Barley guesses that there are no more than twelve actual *Harlequins*. The rest have ended up in the estate sales of deceased library patrons. Between the two of them,

Barley and Skizzy can check out all the *Harlequins* at once.

Skizzy is skeptical. "Here's the problem: Lady Perfume won't let Redwood past the front door."

"I can hold Redwood while you go in."

"I don't know if Redwood will like that." He sends a telepathic query to Redwood. She doesn't like to be touched by anyone except Skizzy. But she also knows how important the poltergeist mission is. She wants to support Skizzy. She wants to help. "All right, Barley. You can take Redwood. But you have to be gentle with her."

"And you have to be gentle with the librarian."

"Deal."

———————————

A burning picture of Fabio's chest rises from the campfire. Skizzy and Redwood whack it from the air. "Take that, you poltergeist."

Barley hands Skizzy the whiskey flask and says, "We'll rack up a lot of library fines for this."

"That's OK. The library can't issue warrants."

Barley snaps a picture of Skizzy poking Redwood at a burning damsel's face. Tomorrow the image will appear on Facebook. The caption will read:

GOT EJECTED FROM THE LIBRARY

SAVED THE LIBRARY'S SOUL

Your Granddad's Firecracker

Winston doesn't know how to tell Grandpa Earl that he's not a particularly horny boy. The old man delights in pointing out attractive legs and breasts of a startling range of ages. Winston, on the other hand, has never been aroused by a sexual fantasy. Despite his fully developed adolescence, his face twisted in disgust the first time he saw an Internet vagina.

For a while Winston thought he might be gay. There are a few boys in his class he finds attractive. Burly Bookman's belly laugh made him a cuddle candidate for a couple of months. Candidate, but never more. Instead Winston found himself more and more deeply drawn to someone else.

If Winston were caught in a zombie movie with only one other living human in the world, he would want his co-survivor to be someone who has experienced enough strange violence to stay calm and focused in the act of decapitating a walking corpse. Someone who has spent detailed hours planning for the possibility of a walking corpse. Someone who has actually hallucinated a walking corpse. To hell with rebuilding the gene pool—Winston wants to spend post-doomsday with Carney Banks.

Even without a zombie pandemic, Winston would like Carney Banks to be with him all the time. He wants to talk to Carney on the phone deep into the night. He wants to take road trips with Carney. He wants to fall asleep on Carney's chest. Although the word makes him wince, Winston admits to himself that he really wants Carney to be his boyfriend. But under no circumstances does he want to have sex. Not with Carney, not with anyone. Never.

Sex is the problem. Other boys seem to obsess over the slightest innuendo, while Winston barely notices the bodies at the swimming pool, male or female. He'd rather open his eyes underwater and pretend to be a jellyfish than steal glances at belly buttons. His sex alarm is muted. However, his brain plays dopamine symphonies when Carney is around.

Winston's Oldsmobile is older than Winston and smells like gasoline. Right now the car is silent in the superstore parking lot. Winston's hands are sweaty on the steering wheel. Carney is not sitting next to him. Instead, Carney's girlfriend Stella seems to be tickling the glove box with her bare toes. Her knees are pressing into her chest. Winston is not sure why she is here.

"Your grandpa's a perv," Stella says.

"I know," Winston replies, "He promised to pay for college if I promise to get laid."

"No doubt he'll want to know the details. Are you going to give them to him?"

Winston shifts in the driver seat. He doesn't like the idea of sitting in a parking lot with Carney's girlfriend. She asked him for a ride to the superstore but when they arrived she didn't get out of the car. Winston opened his door. Stella just kept talking.

Stella's voice is cautious. "So you really are a virgin?"

Winston wants Stella to leave. Go into the store, pick out her wares and come back. Get in the car and accept her ride home in silence, silence, silence. If Stella were a boy he would have told her to shove a porcupine up her ass. But Stella is a girl. And for some baffling reason, girls control the conversation. He therefore responds, "Is it so hard to believe?"

"I heard you and Burly Bookman—"

"What? No. Ew. I'm not—"

"You're not?"

"Why are you asking me this?"

Stella seems to sink into some sort of meditation for a moment. Then she comes alive, for the first time letting her thoughts flow freely into words. "Not long ago, I asked Carney to teach me how to steal. He gave me an experience I will never forget. Now I want to return the favor. There is an experience Carney has never had: he has never been with another guy. He is curious. He wants to know what it's like. Carney likes you, Winston. He considers you his best friend. He's also attracted to you."

Suddenly Winston's mouth is dry. There isn't enough tap in the city's water system to make him feel less parched.

Now there is a hand on his knee. He thinks his knee should probably tingle more than it does.

Now there is breath on his ear. Wow. That does tingle. It tingles more than Winston has ever tingled before. The hair on the back of his neck is rising to meet the air. It's not the intensity of arousal that the boys at the picnic table describe, but it points in the same direction. So this is what it's like to be a mammal.

Stella pulls back into her own space. "So," she says. "Carney and I are hanging out tonight. Care to join us?"

What size firecracker does it take to blow up a mailbox? That is the question that has preoccupied Carney Banks for the past three days. He decided to make a science experiment.

He opened the stash of barely legal explosives he'd stolen from the fireworks tent last July. The M-90 is the most potent ground explosive legally available. It barely packs enough wallop to make Carney's fingers hurt. But taken by the dozen, the powder from the M-90's add together to make a homemade facsimile of a cherry bomb or even an M-80.

The M-80 was designed by the U.S. Military to simulate weapons fire. It was legally sold as a toy when Carney's granddad was a child. As a result, Carney's granddad spent his adult life wearing a glass eye. Though now illegal, the M-80 has a special place in Carney's heart.

Carney began his experiment by lighting a single Black Cat in the mailbox and closing the door. The Black Cat is barely a firecracker at all; even the United States Government considers it safe for children. The result was exactly as expected:

the mailbox stayed closed. Five Black Cats produced the same effect. In fact, neither a pack of one hundred nor even a pack of five hundred Black Cats could blow the lid open on his mom's mailbox. The over-the-counter M-90 did little better.

Time to try the homemade stuff. Carney holds a tennis ball packed with the flash powder from ten M-90's, pricked with a fuse, and resealed with superglue. It is the closest approximation to a true cherry bomb he will ever see. His uncle Fritz, the veteran who spends his life hobbling back and forth across a cabin on Goblin Mountain, gave him the specifications.

Carney places the cherry bomb in the mailbox. The fuse lights. The door closes. A foreign sound overlays the echo of the fuse burning. It's a familiar car engine. Winston!

Winston's Oldsmobile pulls up next to the curb. Stella is leaning out the passenger seat, about to give Carney a kiss on the lips. Carney is moving his hand in a swimming motion, signaling Winston to keep driving. Stella's elbow is inches from the mailbox when the homemade cherry bomb ignites.

The sound is like gunfire. The mailbox door springs open. Smoke appears. Both Stella and Winston jolt. Swearing ensues.

Carney's rage bubbles for a few seconds, just long enough to convince himself that the accident would have been prevented if only Winston had heeded Carney's command to keep driving. Now absolved, Carney surrenders to a full body laugh. He keeps laughing until he doubles over and rolls onto his side, thus disturbing a hill of fire ants. When his laughter lightens, he notices the burning of the fire ants on his thigh. He doesn't care. He scratches the fire ants off his leg and opens his arms to welcome his two favorite people.

Stella is in high gear tonight, thinks Carney as he passes her a bottle of whiskey so cheap even Carney needs a chaser. Stella's face twists as the booze shoots along her tongue. A gulp of Dr Pepper soon puts her in back in control of the conversation. Carney is happily following. Winston seems nervous, but he'll buckle.

Carney hasn't dated many girls. His first girlfriend was so old, and his second so young, that he kept both relationships secret. Then came Juvie. By the time Stella made her theatric entrance into his life, Carney had more or less given up on romance.

Stella is brilliant. She can read a whole novel in a single day and have a conversation about the plot, while Carney can barely make it though a short story. Stella takes high school classes that earn college credit, while Carney sticks to the classes he might be able to pass while tripping acid. Book-smart though she is, Stella can't steal a fucking camera without getting chased across the parking lot. All of these facts are dwarfed by the fact that Stella is hot. No, not just hot. Fucking hot.

So Carney's fucking hot girlfriend wants a threeway with another dude. Carney is okay with that, as long as there is never a penis anywhere inside him. Besides, if Stella wants a threeway with a dude now, she'll probably be open to a threeway with a chick later. Carney's day will come.

Winston, for his part, just wants to leave. Really, wow, yeah. He wants to leave. Carney is showing a hint of sadism. Winston wouldn't be able to handle any sort cruelty from Carney right now. Winston has his own car and his own keys. He should just leave. Just leave. He reaches for his keys.

Oops. Winston's pocket is empty. Carney's eyes are showing off. Carney, the guy who stole the wallet of a billionaire and then carjacked the same billionaire and didn't get put in jail or even questioned for it, barely used a tenth of his skill when he pulled the keys out of Winston's pocket. Carney is now dangling the keys above a freshly poured double shot of tongue-rot whiskey. "You can have your keys, but you have to drink first."

Stella grabs the keys from Carney's hand. "Carney, Winston is your guest. He can leave anytime he wants." She tosses the keys to Winston.

Fury fills Carney's lungs for a breath but quickly subsides. He calls up his famous party smile and soon the party mood fills the room again. Winston isn't fooled. He knows a rage machine when he sees one. It's part of why he is drawn to Carney. It's also why he can't stay here. He mentions that he has to work in the morning and gives Stella a warm goodbye hug.

Winston approaches Carney for a bro-hug. While the two boys are deep in the hug with nothing but their two fully flexed forearms separating their ribcages, Carney decides to give Winston a preview of the evening. He offers to Winston's earlobe: "I have an M-80."

Winston leans back. "You what?"

"Military Eight Zero."

"Where did you get it?"

"I made it."

"That thing you blew up this afternoon wasn't an M-80."

"No, that was a cherry bomb. I haven't lit the M-80 yet. I just packed it this morning. I used the powder from sixty—yeah, six zero—M-90's."

"That'll blow your fucking hand off."

"Yeah, it will. It'll fuck up a mailbox too. Wanna help me blow up my mom's mailbox? Don't worry, I'll find her a new one. We might have to run when my stepdad—"

Carney doesn't get to finish the sentence because Winston's tongue is rolling in Carney's mouth. Saliva leaks onto both of their chins.

Stella performs an unsportsmanlike victory dance.

———————————

Stella's plan is working even more smoothly than she had anticipated. Winston is helping Carney tie a series of little M-90's along a thick fuse. At the end of the fuse is the homemade M-80 that will do all the damage. If all goes as engineered, the show will consist of eight teaser bangs followed by a mailbox-deforming climax. If the boys are true to their body language, they'll be kissing in their underwear shortly thereafter.

Carney is regaling Winston with tales of childhood thievery. Carney's mother taught him that their ancestors had been hunters and gatherers. All the world was a grocery store and all the groceries were free. Then, somewhere along the timeline, greed took over. People began to claim food as property. The food hoarders began charging money for the simple act of eating. Charging money for food is immoral. Animals don't pay for food, so why should humans? In fact, according to Carney's mother, charging for food is more than immoral. It is criminal. Unfortunately the law is written by criminals. Therefore the people who follow the natural law—those who gather food freely from the grocery store—must be careful not to get caught.

Fueled by his mother's philosophy, Carney became a young master at the art of theft. By age seven he was the home's primary breadwinner. When his mother said "Go find us some supper," Carney came back with an appetizer, a family dinner, and dessert.

Carney no longer sees larceny as the act of righteous rebellion in a society of corruption. In fact, he is pretty sure the world would be a better place if nobody ever stole anything. But his understanding of the damage done by theft is small compared to his understanding that stealing is, well, easy. Stealing is as natural to Carney as playing the piano is to a savant. Stealing focuses Carney's attention like no other activity. It saves more money than all the coupons in the Sunday paper. And, let's face it—some people deserve to be stolen from.

Winston is enamored. His smile never wavers. He laughs when things aren't funny.

Part of Stella wants to be jealous. It's clear that Winston would like to replace Stella as Carney's primary nuzzle-buddy. But Stella believes, although her objectivity is questionable, that Carney doesn't return Winston's affection. Even as Carney lays the seduction onto Winston, he chooses natural moments to glance over at Stella with a broadened smile. One time he even winks at her. Stella thinks she understands what he's trying to communicate: *See? Your plan is working. I'm doing this for you.* Stella just hopes he ends up appreciating the experience.

By the time Carney finishes his tale, the mailbox has swallowed enough explosives to deform a tin box. The door is cracked in order to allow the fuse to dangle. Everyone is breathless. Carney offers Winston the honor of lighting the fuse.

Fire happens. Slow burn. The fuse retreats into the mailbox. Carney shuts the door completely. The three young pyrophiles scramble to the ditch across the street. They squat in close formation with Carney in the middle. Stella catches the sight of Winston's nostrils pulling the evaporated sweat from the back of Carney's neck. Taking in the scent. Perfect. Stella slips her fingers around Carney's bicep and squeezes for an endless minute.

Endless.

The first pop should have happened by now. Or should it? Time slows in times of tension. No, really, the cracker should have fired by now. Stella gives Carney a what-the-fuck look. Carney closes his eyes. Silence is everywhere. The first pop—

—happens. All three spectators jolt. Stella's fingernail digs into Carney's arm. Carney drops his hand onto Winston's thigh. Stella counts seven more pops. All the little ones. The mailbox door is shut and the box is not deformed. But the ninth explosion, the big one, the one that could tear off fingers—the M-80—has yet to explode.

Carney gives his scalp a nervous rub. The moments stretch and stretch. No explosion. Carney looks back at Stella. She is genuinely frightened for the second time since he has known her. Winston is fully alert, awaiting Carney's leadership. Carney again looks at the mailbox. The M-80 really should have exploded by now.

Still low to the ground, Carney takes a careful, exaggerated step toward the mailbox. His adrenaline has heightened his senses enough to hear the ambient traffic of Bison Avenue some four blocks away. The M-80 is an enemy. Carney knows how to deal with an enemy. Never back down. Let the enemy know that you're crazier than he is. Keep him guessing. The M-80 is no different. It will back down. Everybody does.

Carney sneaks to the enemy's position. He conjures all of his finesse to open the mailbox door. There is nothing but smoke. Soon the M-80 is visible. The fuse is gone.

As Carney's fingers close around the bomb, a smoldering bit of fuse suddenly finds enough oxygen to ignite the powder.

Big boom.

———————————

Stella will no longer be allowed at Carney's house. Carney's mother finds it easy to blame the new girlfriend for the loss of baby's two fingers. As Carney situates himself in his mother's car, the crazed woman hangs back, poking her finger at Stella's nose, and says, "Do you know he has two other girlfriends? You're not the only slut in his life." Carney's stepdad wraps his firm hands around the woman's shoulders. She pulls back.

Carney's stepdad drives his family to the emergency room. Winston drives Stella.

Sitting in waiting area surrounded by people in even worse shape than Carney, Winston and Stella now watch Carney's mother accompany the bandaged youth into the treatment area. Carney's mother throws one last glare back at Stella before the door swings shut behind her.

Winston speaks softly. He lets Stella know that he'll be "open to the, uh, previous, um, arrangement" as soon as Carney is feeling up to it.

Stella maintains her stare at the swinging door. "I can't believe you just said that. There will be no threesome, Winston. If you want to have sex with Carney, then feel free. But for your own sake, try not to fall in love with him."

As the door swings to a standstill, Winston finds himself wishing he'd been born a reptile.

Bureau of Minor League Affairs

Cheryl Masterson loves lawn day. Each blade of grass, freshly decapitated, saves its own life by whipping up a mix of chemicals that scars the wound, fights infection, alerts its neighbors of impending doom. The grassy cloud floats in the breeze that flows from Cheryl's kitchen window to her living room window. By the time her lawn is fully cut, about 100 gallons of lawn-scented air has made a detour through Cheryl's nostrils. Intoxicating.

When she isn't smelling the lawn, Cheryl is busy being the wife of the town's most successful rental property lord. Jay Masterson is a businessman, ambitious enough to provide comfort for her and their children. All Cheryl has to do is be perfect. And perfect she is: her makeup is fully applied and the heavy fumes of coffee and bacon fight for dominance every morning as Jay's alarm rips him from sleep. Organically grown lunches accompany Gilbert and Michael to school. No stray dust particle dares to show itself on the shiny surfaces around the house. Cheryl is content in her life of quiet contributions, so long as she is able to enjoy her scraps of selftime.

Until recently, Cheryl mowed her own lawn. It was her favorite time of the week, even better than her after-hours dates with *Harlequin Romances*. No matter that the library has never had more than thirteen *Romances* in its collection at a time. She was content to cycle through them, week after week, year after year.

Then, two weeks ago, something terrible happened. Her Sunday trip to the library's romance section revealed an empty *Harlequin* shelf. Mandy, the librarian who smells like she never spends more than $10 on a bottle of perfume, said the *Harlequins* had been checked out by two crazy men who seemed like they were on a mission. Mandy didn't know the nature of the mission, but she suspected she would never see those books again.

Cheryl's life crumbled right there on the library floor. All the quirks of her daily existence, so easily overlooked before, suddenly became unbearable. The thought of Jay's belly, quaking as he thundered some childish complaint about a pimple on his thigh, now seemed like an endless and dreadful future. Gilbert's reruns of fat girl jokes went from adorably oblivious to just plain mean. Michael's saxophone talent, previously one of Cheryl's favorite brag topics, became a vector toward seeing her son sell his belongings and move into a cardboard box under a freeway bridge in Kansas City.

These terrible thoughts followed Cheryl into her minivan. They stopped with her at the Bison Avenue red light. They surrounded her all the way into her garage, clicked their heels with her into the kitchen, and dripped blood out of the chicken she had so lovingly set out to thaw for an ungrateful family. As she sliced the bird, she noticed that the knife seemed to flirt with her fingers. Even when she sliced straight down, the blade moved inward as though it were drawn to her touch.

Her mind played the fantasy of accepting the knife's affection and watching her fingers roll away from her hand and drop into the chicken bowl. She wondered whether her fingers, properly deboned, would have a noticeably different taste or texture than the chicken. Would her family know the difference?

Their tongues might not know the difference between human meat and chicken meat, but at least their eyes would detect her bloody, bandaged, fingerless hand. Or would they? Jay might be too busy complaining about some filthy, lazy, late-for-rent tenant. Gilbert would be staring deep into his cell phone. Michael's headphones would be blasting a musical world into his brain while slowly deafening his eardrums. Cheryl was now convinced that she could use her own blood for salad dressing and not a single member of her family would notice.

The knife kissed her fingertip, bringing her back to attention. *Fingers are still attached*, she thought. *Good. Wow. I'm getting wound up.*

The doorbell introduced the solution. His name is Bryce. She knows his reputation all too well. He is the only athlete at Benjamin High School who can outperform Gilbert. He is a left-handed pitcher who, unlike practically every other pitcher, can also hit the ball. In last year's All-Conference game, Bryce threw a one-hitter and hit two out of the ballpark. His performance earned a mention on ESPN. The shout-out, barely

71

ten seconds long, made the front page of the *Times*. The article is now framed and displayed in the Friends of the Devilhorns Annex at Benjamin High School to remind all the other mothers how little their sons have accomplished.

Bryce's superiority doesn't stop at baseball. He consistently beats Gilbert in the twenty-yard dash. On the football field, Bryce catches nearly every ball Gilbert throws him, even when Gilbert is under pressure and off center.

Kaylie, Bryce's bleach-blond mother who scratches her nose like a cocaine addict, looks for opportunities at PTO meetings to mention every little phone call from every little recruiter.

Cheryl wishes Bryce would fall under a freight train and amputate both of his legs, or at least find a way to graduate early so that Gilbert could take his rightful place as the best athlete in school.

But, two Sundays ago, Bryce had other plans. In addition to being an athlete destined for fame on the college or even the professional circuit, Bryce was now an entrepreneur. He wanted to mow Cheryl's lawn.

Behind her most plastic smile, Cheryl thought, *Fine, you little shit. You little moon eclipsing my son. Service me. Mow my lawn.*

Today is glorious lawn day. Cheryl gets to smell the blood of grass while watching her son's only competition demean himself by accepting her money in exchange for menial labor. Cheryl is reminded of her childhood, playing with Barbie dolls while her big sister Lydia left a trail of sweat behind the lawn mower.

Cheryl hasn't seen or heard from Lydia in years. She doesn't even know whether Lydia is alive. She probably ended, or will end, her life in a dark room completely alone. On the other hand, Lydia probably knows what an orgasm feels like.

Decades ago, on the day Cheryl had her very first period, Lydia stole Mother's attention by announcing to the family that she was pregnant with the child of her Cherokee boyfriend Lucas. Daddy went on a rampage about a halfbreed walking God's earth for all the neighbors to see. Then he became suddenly calm. "Sweetheart," he said. "Think of the child. He'll be bullied all his life. Whites won't accept him. Indians won't accept him. He will have no family, no people, no culture. He'll be all alone." Lydia cried and cried.

The abortion was illegal but available.

Lydia was never the same after that. She and Lucas disappeared before graduation. They somehow ended up in Cambodia without passports and sold pictures of the war to *Life* magazine. Then they disappeared again.

One day the Feds came to Daddy's house. Apparently Lydia and Lucas had been making good in the mescaline business. Last seen in the Colorado Rockies.

All this happened while Cheryl stayed within five miles of the house where she was born. Of course she wouldn't trade her life. She wouldn't give up the comfort her husband provided, and she certainly wouldn't part with her two beautiful boys. But she wished she could live parallel lives: part of her would stay home to be an angel for her family and the other part would find all the danger and adventure the world has to offer, all the danger and adventure her sister chose to experience instead of living a respectable life.

About the time Cheryl had given up on seeing her sister again, Lydia and Lucas showed up at the front door. They smelled like bums.

After a tense, low-volume discussion in the hallway, Cheryl convinced Jay to let the guests stay in the basement entertainment complex until they got on their feet.

Jay reluctantly gave Lucas a job on the maintenance crew. He soon found that Lucas was skilled at patching things on the cheap. Moreover, Lucas was willing to do unlicensed electrical work. A good employee to have.

When his hippie in-laws' welcome wore thin, Jay searched his empire for a family who hadn't paid rent in awhile. He evicted the tenants and moved Lydia and Lucas into the tiny apartment with carpet that smelled like a child's urine.

The in-laws usually managed to pay rent more or less on time.

During the time when Cheryl and Lydia lived in the same town but not the same house, the sisters didn't grow close, exactly, but they did grow closer than they had ever been. Once in a while, when wine was involved, they even had personal conversations.

One night Lydia told Cheryl about the orgy involving the famous musician Cheryl had never heard of.

Another night Lydia spilled baffling details about eating a cactus and shapeshifting into a lizard.

Yet another night Lydia described the morning she gave up her living pre-born child for Daddy. "The practitioner claimed to be a doctor but the operating room was the basement of a shoddy house and lacked even basic cleanliness. The operating table smelled like gasoline. There was blood—so much blood. The guy said the operation was usually bloody, just not that bloody. The last thing he said to me was 'These things happen.'"

On the night of their final wine-sharing, Lydia confessed that despite having no desire to get legally married she and Lucas wanted to conceive another child. They tried, tried, tried and failed, failed, failed. It tore her up inside to know that she was so torn up inside that she would probably never have a living baby.

That same night, quietly, Lydia disappeared again. She didn't quit her job. She didn't settle with her landlord. She didn't even tell her lover. She just left.

Lucas still works for Jay. He still lives in the same smelly apartment. He doesn't talk about Lydia. Jay is okay with that.

Now, sitting at the window, sipping coffee and staring at the overachieving shirtless athlete mowing her lawn, Cheryl wonders whether Lydia would be perverted enough to invite the boy inside. Offer him coffee. Let her housecoat slip during conversation.

When Bryce's mowjob has left a green chessboard pattern on the grass, he walks his muscles to the back door and knocks.

Like last week, Cheryl hands him the check and twinkles him goodbye. But this time he doesn't leave. He just stands there, smiling like he has read her therapist's notebook and knows all her secret addictions.

Cheryl decides to abandon subtlety. "So I'll see you next week, then. Bye!"

"You know, Mrs. Masterson, I'm not due for my next lawn for another hour. I'm also a caffeine addict—who isn't? I can tell you only buy the best coffee. It smells so good!"

Did he just invite himself into my house? That presumptuous little germ sack! But, presumptuous or not, Cheryl can't stand the thought of Kaylie spreading rumors about how Cheryl is too stuck up to let Bryce drink a cup of coffee. "Come on in."

So there he sits at her kitchen table, gabbing like a salesman, trying to regale her with tales of canoes on the river: His buddies Eoff and Kuykendall were in one canoe; Bryce and the beer were in the other. The three buddies stumbled up the cliff and jumped back into the river. Over and over they jumped into shallow water.

On Bryce's third jump, his sense of time must have slipped. He felt like he should have hit the water but he was still in the air. So, jaw agape, he looked down to see how far away the water was. As soon as he did so, the water uppercut his jaw, knocking his bottom teeth into his top teeth and bouncing his jaw back open.

The water was too shallow for jumping, but Bryce had known that already. He knew how to bend his knees to absorb the impact. Then, knees bent, he knew how to launch himself back to the surface.

Things got weird at the surface. His arms and legs were in perfect working order, so treading water was no problem. His neck and jaw, however, would not move. His head was stuck in the knocked-back position and his jaw was stuck fully open.

He remained there, treading water, unable to level himself to swim back to the rocks.

While Eoff and Kuykendall shouted to know whether he was alright, Bryce considered the horrible thought that his neck might be paralyzed. Then, as quickly as the impact hit, the injury faded away. His neck returned to its full range of motion and his jaw regained its ability to flap and flap and flap.

But not everything returned as before. As he swam to the rocks Bryce felt a grittiness between his molars, as though he were crunching sand. He ran his tongue over his teeth (as he tells the story, Bryce opens his mouth and shows Cheryl his tongue sliding back and forth across his teeth) and realized that small chunks of his molars were missing. (He hooks the side of his mouth with his index finger and shows her the chips in his molars. *Well*, thinks Cheryl, *at least he brushes his teeth*.)

As Bryce transitions into the Devilhorn Hardball hazing ritual—it involved spanking and, for some reason, Crisco—Cheryl becomes suddenly aware of his body language. He is leaning forward, talking with his hands as though he would like to touch her arm but is afraid to make the move. On those rare times when he stops talking long enough to breathe, he inhales slowly and fully as though he is taking in her scent. Yes, that is exactly what he is doing. The little snot rag is hitting on her.

At some point he must have used one foot to kick off the other shoe. His sweaty, grass-soaked instep is now pressing upward into her calf. And he's still talking.

As Bryce prattles about the time Eoff used Kuykendall's Ford to pull down an abandoned barn, Cheryl begins a mental letter to Bryce's mother:

Dear Kaylie,

Your filthy son just tried to stick his pecker in me. You know, the little wee-wee you washed in tepid water all those years ago. I'm sure it peed on you at least once. Now it's mostly fully grown and it's pointing at me. Wouldn't you just hate me if I—

——————————————

Cheryl Masterson's yard is more artistically sculpted than any other yard in town. The bushes have been carved into cubic stacks of spheres. The flowerbeds are arranged in a rainbow color pattern. The Homeowners' Association would fine Cheryl for gaudiness (a punishable offense under Article VI, Section iii of the Homeowners' Covenant) if not for the fact that the yardwork appears to have cost a lot of money.

Bryce Bunyan, the aspiring professional baseball player and fully professional lawn sculpting specialist, has found the Masterson yard to be a source of inspiration and creativity. He returns to the yard two or three times per week.

Cheryl has begun to wish Bryce would stay away. Of course he is fun to play with—that is a given. He sometimes comes inside her, stays hard, and comes inside her again. And unlike her husband, Bryce is a reasonably decent kisser. Unfortunately, Bryce doesn't understand discretion. He confessed that he'd told

Eoff and Kuykendall about her, though he swore that he hadn't revealed her name.

Moreover, he has become more and more presumptuous. He appears without calling, shows off his muscles as he walks through the back door like he lives in the house, pours himself some coffee, and rambles to Cheryl about his meaningless daily conquests until Cheryl shuts him up by pressing her finger to his lips or creeping a toe into the leg of his shorts.

The ritual has become routine. The more routine it becomes, the less worth the risk. Every playtime is a roll of the die.

What if Jay comes home early? Jay's obsession with work makes that a rare event, but it does happen. A far more frequent occurrence is that he stays out well past supper. Sometimes he comes home smelling like Jennifer Lopez's signature brand of perfume. It would serve him right to catch his wife in bed with a younger, more attractive man who actually enjoys and appreciates her touch.

But then what? Marriage counseling? The D-word? Her dirty secret laid bare on the courthouse steps? Prison? And what would her boys think of her?

If Jay catches her and takes the story public then the judge will take her boys and send her away. Especially if Piscetty is presiding. Cheryl is pretty sure that Jay and Piscetty shared a hooker in Vegas. The story about the hotel maid stealing both of their wallets just didn't ring true. Having your wallet stolen by a hooker in Vegas is the sort of sick bond that makes men stick together. Piscetty will do whatever Jay asks him to do.

If Jay catches her and goes public, she loses. End of story. Therefore Cheryl needs a safeguard: something to guarantee that even if Jay catches her, he keeps the argument private.

First step: Record Jay's browser history. He is, after all, stupid enough to look at incest-themed Tumblr porn without learning how to cover up his tracks.

Second step: Hire an investigator to watch his every move. Cheryl has the money. After years of scraping off the top of shopping trips, she has accumulated quite the stash.

She might not be able to withstand the truth in a court of law, but she can certainly outwit her husband. That's one reason she married him.

But is it worth it? Sure, every orgasm is a ecstatic fuck-you to Kaylie, but is Cheryl willing to throw chaos into her comfortable life just to continue playing body games with the irritatingly talkative but divinely built boy who, at this very moment, is drilling his tongue into her vagina?

"A little to the left," she instructs.

Bryce's tongue moves the wrong way.

"No, not to your left. To my left."

Bryce looks directly into her eyes and says, "Yes, Mommy."

Everything stops. "Did you just call me Mommy?"

Bryce is flustered. He apologizes with a hint of groveling.

Now would be the perfect time to end it. Tell him how disgusted she feels. Tell him that he needs to see a therapist. Having seen nearly a dozen therapists herself, she can recommend one.

Wait. No. Bad idea. Any therapist would be bound by law to report her. So how does she end it?

As risky as every playdate is, ending the relationship is the most dangerous act of all. Bryce holds all the cards. If he retaliates by tattling, then he is at once a victim and a stud. Cheryl, on the other hand, is divorced, estranged from her boys, ostracized from the community, and quite possibly spending her middle years in jail.

Ending the relationship may be delicate, she decides, *but we have to stop. This has gone too far.* Her determination is strong enough to end it right now, if not for a nagging little problem: she hasn't gotten off yet.

Cheryl looks the kid in the eye. "Get back down there."

Apparently relieved, the kid obeys.

His hair is barely long enough to grab, but she manages. Cheryl pulls his head back. "I didn't hear a 'Yes, Mommy.'"

The kid smiles a dirty, dirty smile.

Bryce's cunnilingual skills find manic inspiration. His tongue is a telepathic vibrator. It conjures the exact force, frequency and location necessary to intensify her body's quaking and quaking and quaking until—

The orgasm rattles the walls. The mirror reflects the scream that begins in her clit and resonates between her vagina and her mouth. Her climax climaxes all previous climaxes.

As Bryce climbs on top of her to kiss her taste back into her mouth, a chilling sound reflects through the house. The front door has opened.

The lovers panic. In her haste to get out of bed, Cheryl smacks Bryce's face with her shoulder. Bryce jerks back, falls to the floor, and scampers to find his scattered clothes.

Footfalls fill the hallway.

Cheryl hisses, "Get into the bathroom. Hide!"

The kid does not obey. Having donned his shorts and grabbed his shoes, he lets the rest go. Shirtless and barefoot, he runs into the hallway, dances around the giant man he thinks would like to attack him, and disappears out the front door.

The giant man in the hallway makes it to the bedroom door and stops. It is not Jay. Rather, it is Jay's most trusted cheapskate handyman and Lydia's former lover / hippie non-husband / Cherokee boyfriend / open-relationship shack-up Lucas. "Cute kid," he says. "Is he bi?"

Cheryl covers her nudity with bedsheets and her terror with righteousness. "Didn't your mother teach you how to knock?"

"Sorry. Tipis don't have doors."

"Cherokees don't live in tipis. Never did."

"No, we live in shitty apartments owned by your husband. Speaking of whom: Jay sent me to fetch the electrician's kit. I'm going to install circuit breakers at Ben Creek. The fire marshal is demanding code compliance all of the sudden. I figure Jay must have beaten him at golf. So here I stand: the unlicensed electrician. I do love breaking the law, especially in the service of a pillar-of-the-community family like yours."

"Please don't tell Jay. Please?"

"Your sex life is none of my business. Unless, of course, you're still in the mood. It would be the first time I've ever done a woman and her sister both. It's on my to-do list."

"I'd rather go to prison."

"Your loss. Once you go Indian, you never go—wait. What

rhymes with Indian? Oh, look! Boxers." Lucas reaches into the corner and picks up a pair of flannel boxers that are several sizes too small to be Jay's. He holds them to his face and pulls a long, slow breath through the fabric. "The kid sweats a lot. Good pheromones. I'll keep these as a souvenir. You know, Cheryl, I misjudged you. I've always known you were a freak. I just didn't think you knew."

"I am not a—" but she can't finish the sentence, at least not with certainty. Instead she says, "Just go, Lucas. Please."

"Okie-dokie. I suppose I've tortured you for long enough. Welcome to the criminal class, Cheryl." Lucas turns his big frame westward and he walks on down the hall.

Pinswinger

My name is Pinswinger the Bowling Ball. Other bowling balls fear me.

The synapses in my armslave's brain have grown into a web of wide-flowing currents that tense and relax his muscles in the perfect combination with the perfect timing to spin me sliding into ten pins at once. The whole of his organism—every cell—knows exactly what to do, twelve times in a row, game after game, each throw exactly as before. Any variation costs me the game.

I don't lose well. For example, if I had any mass at all besides my polyurethane inner core and reactive resin skin—that is, if I had, say, arms and legs—then I'd walk right up to the drunk hippie named Barley Hopps and plop my boneshattering body onto his pinky toe. Barley Hopps, who failed to notice that the entire bowling alley had gone silent when my armslave began my backswing. As the swing reached its highest point, the drunk hippie, either mindlessly or maliciously, felt it was the perfect time to basketball-shoot an empty beer can into the trash container. The sound echoed throughout the alley and distracted my armslave enough to tense, ever so slightly, his right deltoid muscle. My armslave threw me a fraction of the width of

85

the hippie's dreadlock to the left. Sensing his error mid-swing, my armslave compensated by stealing some spin. I therefore hit the headpin nearly head-on, resulting in the mother of all splits: the seven-ten split that looks like the two back molars in in the mouth of a meth addict.

My armslave went out proud. Even the back molar split is no match for him. He threw me with such precision that I knocked one back molar into the other. The audience clapped and my armslave took a slight bow. Our dignity was salvaged. Our score was not.

Barley Hopps reacted as though he were unaware of his blunder.

Of course my armslave could have retaliated by smashing the hippie's forehead onto the waxed floor, but only at the cost of our career. I, meanwhile, was constrained by physics. Lacking any physical power whatsoever I was forced to use my only means of interacting with the world. I used telepathy.

Late that night I reached out to locate the drunk hippie's mind and found him in his girlfriend's bed fondling the gauges in her ears. I sifted through his memories for the most horrific flashback I could conjure. I then sent him a little pulse of perception that caused him to misinterpret his surroundings.

Barley saw his girlfriend's left ear shapeshift into the female end of an infinitely tangled garden hose. Barley was back in the workroom at the county jail standing next to White Knight Ruck, a man who wasn't exactly gay but who, in the absence of women, liked to sodomize soft men. Barley and the angry sodomite were under orders to untangle the hose under pain of pissing off an authority figure who thought of them both as animals.

A gregarious man, Barley sometimes has difficulty controlling his urge to say what is on his mind. There, in the closest place to Hell he has ever known, internally shouting at himself to shut the fuck up as his mouth opened to share his excitement that he would be a free man in less than a week, no, please stop, never *never* brag about your release date, Barley's imprisoned better judgment watched helplessly as his freely speaking mouth made vibrations in the air that sounded like "I can't believe I'm gonna get laid this weekend. After eleven months, finally!"

White Knight Ruck didn't look up, but his bone-sharp knuckles flew with perfect aim into Barley's teeth, jolting his vision and knocking his skull backward into the wall.

The flashback lasted just long enough for present-day Barley to belt out his most mammalian survival scream and skip over the thought process that would lead him to straighten his finger before pulling it out of the gauged hole in his girlfriend's earlobe. Instead, he yanked his finger back, still hooked. Her skin broke, and the girl faced the brief but real possibility that Barley had pulled part of her ear off.

Barley did not get laid that night.

While Barley Hopps was making his girlfriend's ear bleed, my armslave took comfort in the arms of his lover. Shandy is a good woman. She is the first lover who hasn't tried to convince my armslave that he spends too much time with me. The first lover who hasn't acted visibly sad when he takes me to practice day after day. The only lover I haven't chosen to drive away.

At her behest, my armslave left me in the bowling bag for an entire day. Shandy had suggested a night on the town to take his mind off the loss, and then a fresh start at practice tomorrow.

As much as being cooped up in the bowling bag made me want to make Shandy hallucinate swimming like a cockroach in a flushing toilet, I showed restraint. I had to admit that her logic was sound. My armslave needed a break.

Being left in the bowling bag always makes me restless. I passed the time by peeking into my armslave's evening, both from his eyes and from Shandy's. Turns out they're both lousy dancers. They flailed their arms into one another and smacked enough other dancers that a radius of empty floor opened around them. They wiggled, kissed, and spilled drinks on each other.

When I was satisfied that my armslave's recreation was adequate to refocus our game, I peeked into my rival bowling ball's practice. I tried to make his armslave miss the strike but the ball was using its full concentration to protect his armslave from my influence.

When I finally got bored with my failed attempts at sabotage, I decided to check in on Barley Hopps. Barley was sharing a beer with his homeless friend Skizzy in a bar that smelled like a beer-soaked ashtray. Barley was telling Skizzy how vivid and realistic his jail flashback had been. "And the thing is," said Barley, "I was completely sober except for the beer and weed." Barley was cute in his bafflement. Of course, he had no idea that his hallucination had been induced by any kind of outside force, to say nothing of a bowling ball. He feared that his decade of swallowing every hallucinogen that passed in front of him might be having a cumulative effect.

Moreover, Barley was irritated because it seemed that Skizzy was more interested in the beer, which Barley had purchased, than in Barley's story. Skizzy's only advice: "It was a hallucination. You've had them before. Deal with it."

"Yeah, but I only had them before when I was tripping. Last night I was sober."

"You're always tripping. Your whole life is a trip. It just seems real because it mostly follows the laws of physics. Sober or not, there's only one rule of hallucinating: flow with it. Don't fight it."

"Skizzy, I had a flashback to the year I spent in jail. I don't want to think about that time ever again."

"Yes, yes. Jail sucks. It sucks for you, it sucks for me; it sucks for everyone. And now you have to process all those emotions because apparently you're a lesbian. Can we get another beer?"

This Skizzy seemed fascinating so I sifted through his memories. I found them even more nonlinear and disjointed than most humans'. He saw brighter colors than most. His brain, even more than most, excelled at creating patterns out of random data.

Looking through Skizzy's eyes in a memory, I saw men in masks breaking into a locked bedroom where he was sleeping. They were looking for a shipment of medicine. Wait—not medicine. Drugs. I get those words confused. They beat him with cute little sticks, wrapped his body in tape made of ducks, and left him in the bathtub.

I couldn't put his memories in chronological order, except for those times when he was physically smaller. While I was nosing through his childhood, Skizzy jolted. He then turned back to Barley. "Did you go to the bowling alley last night?"

"Yeah, there was an exhibition match with a couple of pros. The girl I was telling you about—she's really cool and has sexy gauges, but for some reason she likes professional bowling."

"I guess you drank a bunch of beer?"

"Obviously. How else could I stand being in a bowling alley?"

"Yeah, well, you chucked a beer can at the trashcan and distracted one of the pros mid-swing. Cost him the game."

"I don't think it was me. I think the bowler—"

"Yeah, it was you."

"Wait—how did you even know about that?"

Good question. How did he know about that?

"The bowling ball told me."

No, I didn't.

"Yes, you did."

No, I didn't.

"Don't you think I can hear you poking around in my head, you bitter old gutter licker?"

Barley asked whether Skizzy had taken his meds today.

"If I'd taken my meds, do you think I'd be talking to a bowling ball?"

I was taken by surprise. I'd never been noticed by a human before. I'd been noticed by other bowling balls, of course. Hell, I'd waged psychic warfare against a dozen. The bowling balls knew what going on, but the armslaves never did.

Skizzy, on the other hand, sensed my presence. It occurred to me that if he could feel me in his head then he might be able to follow me. He might be able to alter my perception and sabotage my game.

I panicked. I had nothing against Skizzy but I was in the unfamiliar position of wanting to flee. I felt like I needed to do some damage before I did. I needed to convince Skizzy not to come poking around for me.

I sifted through his memories and found a particularly humiliating one. I sent him a perception pulse. His surroundings at the Horndevil Pub morphed into the playground at Ben Creek Park. Young Skizzy's stepbrother Billy was twisting Skizzy's arm behind him. Skizzy felt the pain shooting from his arm down his back. Screaming wasn't helping, but Skizzy knew what would.

With his one free hand, Skizzy reached behind him and felt his brother's bare knee. Skizzy slid his fingers upward into the leg of Billy's shorts. Somewhere around mid-thigh was a switch made of nerve endings that turned Billy's mood from platonic sadism to a relatively gentle lust. If he could reach the switch then his brother would undergo a series of predictable changes. Every part of Billy's body would freeze. His breathing would deepen as his circulation shifted. He'd show an immediate desire for silence. *Shhhh,* he would say, *stop screaming. Someone might hear. There. I let go of your arm. See? Now be quiet. Let's go to the sewer tunnels. You want to? Yeah, you do. Let's go play.*

But in order to reach the switch Skizzy had to get his fingers a few inches higher into Billy's shorts. Billy wasn't letting him budge.

Then something remarkable happened. I was no longer making Skizzy's memory come alive for him. Rather, I was reliving Skizzy's memory from my own eyes, as though I actually had eyes and arms and a face. One of my arms was in terrible pain. I also had real liquid emotions. The desire to disappear into a dark, quiet place was eclipsed by the irrational certainty that my life was in danger. I think it's what the armslaves call fear.

Billy tightened the hold on my arm and sent lightning bolts of pain across my body as I tried with increasing desperation to sneak my fingers up his shorts.

Then Billy let go. For a brief moment I thought I was free. But then the open palm of his hand smacked into my ear, causing me to lose my balance and fall to the ground. I rolled over to face him and saw that my attacker was no longer Billy. It was Skizzy. He had taken this dream over.

Skizzy fell, full body weight, onto his knees. His knees in turn jabbed into my pelvis, just straddling my underdeveloped groin. His giant hands held my shoulders to the ground.

Skizzy spat when he talked. "You think you can scare me with a little hallucination, Pinswinger? I eat hallucinations for breakfast. Now get out of my head and leave Barley Hopps alone or I'll melt your perception so much you'll accidentally make your armslave drop you on his foot. His bones will shatter. Then you'll spend the next ten weeks in the bowling bag."

I had never been vulnerable before. I had never felt pain. I wanted it to stop but I couldn't give up. I had to make some sort of counter-demand. I had to salvage my dignity if not my score. I screamed back at him, "Then tell Barley Hopps to stay away from my armslave!"

Skizzy said, "It's a deal," and then everything was dark. I no longer felt pain. I no longer had arms. I was back to my old self: a typical sixteen-pound telepathic bowling ball, maybe a little meaner than most.

For the first time in my life, I was happy to be in the bowling bag. I didn't envy humans for their eyesight or mobility or sex. I felt no desire to crawl from one human mind to another, drinking their lives and tripping them up for my amusement. Instead, I simply took comfort in the darkness.

Tomorrow my armslave will bring me into the light. I will make sure love flows through his veins. As for Barley Hopps, I'd like more assurance than Skizzy's word that Barley will stay away.

Maybe I can convince Barley's girlfriend that she doesn't really like professional bowling. Maybe I can implant the idea that professional bowling is boring, and that only someone of canine intelligence would enjoy watching a man throw a ball the exact same way twelve times in a row. It's a tough sell, I know. Then again, I am a master illusionist. I just might be able to pull it off.

Lord of the Finger

Marcus Carl and Ina Carol have been married for too long to consider themselves separate human beings. Their bodies have aged in a complementary way: Marcus Carl is like-to-near blind but can hear pretty well, whereas Ina Carol's eyes are sprightly but she can't hear any pitch higher than a freight train. Marcus Carl has the vigorous ability to reach the top shelf, while Ina Carol is flexible enough to squat. Together they ingest enough calories to sustain a single healthy adult.

If you were to walk the shoulder of the little town highway next to their house, you might conclude that Marcus Carl and Ina Carol share lives of rage and abuse. Booming yells, repeated demands, bangs, thumps, and cries for assistance escape the window from sunup to sundown.

Fortunately, these sounds carry no violence. Marcus Carl cracks and topples what he can't see. He yells because it's the only way Ina Carol can hear him. Ina Carol yells because it's the only way to hear herself.

Marcus Carl and Ina Carol may keep the decibel meter lit up in the daytime, but their next-door neighbors keep the volume high at night. Although the next-door housemates are not in any way related, they have all changed their family names to Fingerlord, which is also the name of their rock band. The band's influences include Beethoven, a shoe in a tumble dryer, and a screeching demon.

If Marcus Carl had his way, the members of Fingerlord would each, one by one, be impaled on the finger of the Lord. Or at least be locked in a drunk tank until their musical instruments could fuel a bonfire.

Ina Carol, for her part, loves Fingerlord. Their drum riffs penetrate the only frequency range that can still vibrate her eardrums. Their practices lullaby her to sleep.

One sunny Sunday, Ina Carol decides to express her affection for Fingerlord in the best way she knows how: through baked goods. She gets her doctor-prescribed exercise by walking laps around the kitchen while a baker's pride of cookies smells up the house.

When the baking is done, Marcus Carl snorts. "How come the hellions get cookies but I don't?"

Ina Carol walks the finished product right by him. "You don't need cookies. You're diabetic."

"I'll be diabetic until I die. I might as well eat some cookies."

"Cookies will kill you. And you're not allowed to die. Not until I die. And I ain't ready to die. I got too many cookies to bake." With that, she takes her masterpiece out the door.

———————

Lisa Razormop Fingerlord is the lead singer, guitarist, lyricist, road manager and motivational dictator for the only post-punk thrashadelic glitter-vomit rock band in Benjamin. She managed to book the town's only three stages, but none of them will let Fingerlord return for an encore performance. She was therefore forced to search the surrounding towns for more enlightened venues.

She finally found a willing pizza shop in Garfield, some fifty miles away. The owner has offered to rearrange some tables in order to create enough empty floor space to mimic a stage. He is even willing to pay for gas.

The news of a paid gig has sparked new excitement in the band and renewed authority in the voice of Lisa. "If we don't practice every night between now and Monday, the Muse will drill holes in our eardrums."

The quality of music during the first night's practice begins cold, peaks around eleven, then falls inversely to the drummer's blood alcohol content.

When beats become unfollowable, Lisa grumbles something about a lack of artistic discipline pissing off the Muse. She declares the music portion of the night finished. Music gives way to straight-up alcohol, followed by people yelling at each other for reasons they won't remember in the morning. Vomiting, and suddenly

————————————

the sun is making a horrible fiery slit in the aluminum curtains.

Boom Back Fingerlord lays with his body crumpled on a beanbag. Deep inside an alcohol-amplified dream, Boom Back is living life as a squid. He uses all of his tentacles to pound a 128-piece drumset in front of a stadium of naked and adoring fans. How big is that drumset? Look again! The drums are infinite, Boom Back's arms are infinite, and so is the crowd. A dreadlocked girl, clothed only in tattoos and a hoola hoop, her breasts pressing against the stage, throws him a bundle of flowers, and then a beer (which he catches with one tentacle, thank you!) and finally a boot that hits him in the forehead. Ouch! Why would she throw a boot? Wait—she didn't. The boot is not a dream boot, but rather a real-life physical boot. It smells like Lisa.

"Boom Back!" Definitely Lisa. "Someone's knocking. The Muse wants you to get the door."

"Tell the Muse to deepthroat my drumstick."

Another boot hits him in the head. He responds, "You're out of boots."

Lisa lets slip the demon screech, her signature sound that got her kicked out of every venue in Benjamin. Each of the other bandmates grabs the nearest potential projectile. A volley of unknown items lobs through the lone sunbeam toward Lisa's voice.

Defeated, Lisa drags her headache to the front door, cracks the daylight and faces the terrible noon.

A fury of light invades Lisa's eyes. She considers for a moment that she might still be asleep and squinting her way through a horrible dream. Then again, she might be dead.

Ina Carol recognizes the look. She knows what it's like not to be seen. She makes herself known by belting out a sentence loudly enough to startle a rockstar. "I just love your music! You kids should make a record!"

And then there are cookies.

As the sun hangs red over the western hills, the members of Fingerlord rise from their slumbers. Marcus Carl and Ina Carol have not quite gone to bed. Thus, there is a small window of time that is experienced in the awakened state by both households.

Marcus Carl is spritzing his garden when he hears someone come out of the Fingerlord house. *Well*, he thinks. *They're up early.* He squints and tries to decipher who is on the Fingerlord porch. It's not the girl with the neon hair. He can see neon pretty well. It's not the boy with the chin that looks like a broom. It might be the kid with the tattoos crawling up his face. Or the boy who thinks it's okay to be a girl.

The Fingerlord door slams again. Now there are more of them. Four of the little shits in all. They are yelling at each other. Something about the Muse. What miserable lives! As far as Marcus Carl is concerned, they deserve their misery. His forced insomnia traces the nightly evolution of the drummer's blood alcohol content. That boy drinks too much.

Marcus Carl decides to get their attention. He clangs his spritzer bottle onto a can of WD-40 and drops both into an empty Folgers can, creating such a racket that all four band members stop yelling and look toward him. Marcus Carl raises his right fist above his head. He then raises his middle finger above his fist.

The neon girl responds by screaming like a demon.

Neon hair! What self-respecting man lets his daughter wear neon hair? The girl no doubt has at least three boyfriends and brags about her upcoming abortion. She probably dropped out of school after seducing some poor young teacher. Marcus Carl shakes his head. Girls like that didn't exist when he was a kid.

Now, don't get the wrong idea. The girls in his generation weren't prudes. They really weren't. Some of them played the kissing game. Some even met boys behind McLeod's barn for some old-fashioned hanky panky. What memories! But that was different: those girls didn't talk openly about hanky panky, they didn't dress like they were in the mood for hanky panky, and most importantly: they didn't have neon hair.

————————————

Ina Carol is already sleeping when the kids begin their third consecutive night of racket. Marcus Carl tries to keep the drums out of his head but he can't. He has finally had enough. It's time to call the law.

Marcus Carl uses his calories to maneuver himself to the side table in the kitchen, which has been the home of the rotary telephone for the past forty years.

Under different circumstances, there is a certain confusion that happens after the death of a loved one. When you walk through your dead mother's house, you intensely expect to see her in her usual place. Sometimes, for a moment, you actually see her sitting on her dining room throne, loyally smoking her cigarette, looking out the window as though nothing extraordinary has happened.

Marcus Carl has a similar experience with the telephone. His cloudy eyes tell his brain that the telephone is exactly where it ought to be. He reaches out to pick it up. Only when his fingers close on cold air does he realize that the telephone is gone.

Unlike the neon girl next door, Marcus Carl has not practiced the art of screaming like a demon. But when he realizes that his access to the telephone—the comfort line to his protectors, sympathizers and therapists at the police station—has gone missing, he screams a scream that would make Lisa Fingerlord jealous. He screams a scream that even Ina Carol can hear, even in her sleep.

Ina Carol went to sleep expecting to be awakened. Now that her husband's vocal alarm has sounded, she doesn't feel like using her calories to walk into the kitchen. Instead, she lets her husband's fury fuel his journey to the bedroom.

"Ina Carol! Where on God's earth is the telephone?"

Ina Carol pretends to be partially asleep. "Be quiet, Love. I'm listening to music."

"Music! You call that music? The walls are shaking!"

"It's what the kids listen to nowadays."

"I ain't a kid and neither are you. Now get me the phone so I can call the law."

"I don't remember where I put it. C'mon, Marcus Carl. Crawl into bed with me. Let's pretend we're kids again. Let's pretend we're behind McLeod's barn."

"You're just encouraging them, Ina Carol. Helping the world slip."

Ina Carol pats the bed. "Ain't nothin' you can do about the world." She shoots him the look that, once upon a time, caused his trousers to swell at church. And also at his mother's dinner table. Not to mention the soda table at the drug store.

Marcus Carl grumbles and considers his options. He can either yell at his wife, which a lifetime of marriage has proven pointless, or he can involve himself in some rarely offered old-fashioned hanky panky.

Marcus Carl checks the nightstand drawer. Lube? Check. Blue pills? Expired. Better take two. He swallows the pills and slides into bed with an unusual amount of grace. He holds his wife as tightly as her bones will allow. He holds her with the full awareness that she is the only reason he still clings to this life.

As he waits for the pills to spread through his blood, Marcus Carl notices the rhythms in the room. As usual, Marcus Carl takes longer, deeper breaths than Ina Carol. However, as the minutes pass, their breaths reach out to one another, looking for connection. Each lover breathes more like the other until they are respiring as a single organism. Eventually their collective breathing falls into time with the drunk drumbeats, imperfect as geriatric heartbeats, that are penetrating the wall.

Absorbed in the harmonics of lover, breath, and drum, the old man has an epiphany. For the first time since the invention of rock and roll, Marcus Carl almost understands the young generation's music.

Almost.

Previous appearances of these stories

"Cocky Jockroach," "Reading is bad for you," "Jesus Jill Snares the Soul," and "Carney's Stellar Banana Trip" first appeared in chapbook *Benjamin Golden Devilhorns* (2009). "Earl and the Gas-poop Sketty" first appeared in the chapbook *Comet Hillbilly-Bopp* (2003).

About the author

Doug Shields was born in a Kansas town that was built and abandoned by the railroad. During a queer puberty he was moved to an Arkansas town famous for its KKK headquarters. From there, he left to find peace at the Arkansas School for Mathematics and Sciences.

After high school he earned a physics degree and founded Houston Poetry Slam at the art commune known as *southmorehouse*. He then returned to the Ozarks, served as Slammaster of Fayetteville, and attended graduate school in physics. He produced and hosted *High On Words Radio*, the premier spoken word show on KXUA-FM.

Doug has published five screen-printed poetry posters and numerous chapbooks, one of which has earned a Pushcart Prize nomination. He now lives in Fayetteville, Arkansas, where he is the Chief Executive Artist for the spoken word entertainment company GigaPoem, LLC.

GigaPoem.com
a community of WordCraft

If you enjoyed this book, please help support it by rating it on Amazon, Goodreads, and any other online forum.

And we hope you'll go to saltimbanquebooks.com and sign up for our mailing list.

Thanks!

ALSO FROM SALTIMBANQUE BOOKS:

THE VICTIM (AND OTHER SHORT PLAYS), by J. Boyett

In *The Victim*, April wants Grace to help her prosecute the guys who raped them years before. The only problem is, Grace doesn't remember things that way.... Also included: A young man picks up a strange woman in a bar, only to realize she's no stranger after all; An uptight socialite learns some outrageous truths about her family; A sister stumbles upon her brother's bizarre sexual rite; A first date ends in grotesque revelations; A love potion proves all too effective; A lesbian wedding is complicated when it turns out one bride's brother used to date the other bride.

RICKY, by J. Boyett

Ricky's hoping to begin a new life upon his release from prison; but on his second day out, someone murders his sister. Determined to find her killer, but with no idea how to go about it, Ricky follows a dangerous path, led by clues that may only be in his mind.

BROTHEL, by J. Boyett

What to do for kicks if you live in a sleepy college town, and all you need to pass your courses is basic literacy? Well, you could keep up with all the popular TV shows. Or see how much alcohol you can drink without dying. Or spice things up with the occasional hump behind the bushes. And if that's not enough you could start a business....

COMING IN SUMMER 2015:

COLD PLATE SPECIAL, by Rob Widdicombe

Jarvis Henders has finally hit the beige bottom of his beige life, his law-school dreams in shambles, and every bar singing to him to end his latest streak of sobriety. Instead of falling back off the wagon, he decides to go take his life back from the child molester who stole it. But his journey through the looking glass turns into an adventure where he's too busy trying to guess what will come at him next, to dwell on the ghosts of his past.

STEWART AND JEAN, by J. Boyett

A blind date between Stewart and Jean explodes into a confrontation from the past when Jean realizes that theirs is not a random meeting at all, but that Stewart is the brother of the man who once tried to rape her. Or is she the woman who murdered his brother? And will anyone ever know?

THE LITTLE MERMAID: A HORROR STORY, by J. Boyett

Brenna has an idyllic life with her heroic, dashing, lifeguard boyfriend Mark. She knows it's only natural that other girls should have crushes on the guy. But there's something different about the young girl he's rescued, who seemed to appear in the sea out of nowhere—a young girl with strange powers, and who will stop at nothing to have Mark for herself.

I'M YOUR MAN, by F. Sykes

It's New York in the 1990's, and every week for years Fred has cruised Port Authority for hustlers, living a double life, dreaming of the one perfect boy that he can really love. When he meets Adam, he wonders if he's found that perfect boy after all … and even though Adam proves to be very imperfect, and very real, Fred's dream is strengthened to the point that he finds it difficult to awake.

THE UNKILLABLES, by J. Boyett

Gash-Eye already thought life was hard, as the Neanderthal slave to a band of Cro-Magnons. Then zombies attacked, wiping out nearly everyone she knows and separating her from the Jaw, her half-breed son. Now she fights to keep the last remnants of her former captors alive. Meanwhile, the Jaw and his father try to survive as they maneuver the zombie-infested landscape alongside time-travelers from thirty thousand years in the future.... Destined to become a classic in the literature of Zombies vs. Cavemen.